# WITHOUT YOU

## DELANEY DIAMOND

Garden Avenue Press

Looking at the monitor in the kitchen, Charisse Burrell saw when her ex-husband's black Range Rover pulled in front of the three-car garage of her six-bedroom, seven-bath house north of the city. She tossed the dish towel onto the counter and rushed to the door, swinging it open as her kids traipsed up the steps to the front door.

They poured into the house with duffel bags in tow—seventeen-year-old Ennis, her ten-year-old, Terrence Junior, and the youngest, eight-year-old Chelsea. Her ex-husband, Terrence, sauntered in behind them and closed the door.

Charisse hugged each of her kids in turn, as if she hadn't seen them in months instead of the few days their father had taken them to Miami for the weekend. She left the biggest hug for Chelsea since the boys were no longer as affectionate as they used to be when they were her age.

"Hi, Mommy!" said Chelsea, a lanky eight-year-old with colorful clips at the end of her braids that made each one swing around her little face.

She dropped a kiss to her daughter's forehead. "How's my little princess today?"

Chelsea was going through a stage where she called

herself a princess, and her ex-husband didn't help by gifting her with tiaras, which she wore every chance she could. She wore one right now. Along with the Tiffany-blue miniature bridesmaid dress under her jacket and the white shoes she wore, she certainly looked the part of a princess at the moment.

"I'm fine. Tired," Chelsea replied.

"I bet you are. I'm sure Daddy kept you busy all weekend. Okay you guys, go ahead and put away your bags. You know the drill," Charisse called as she followed the boys, who'd lumbered down the hall.

Charisse made her way back to the kitchen with Terrence and Chelsea following.

The kitchen was a wide open space and the heart of the house, filled with top-of-the-line appliances that included two ovens and a Sub-Zero refrigerator filled with all manner of beverages and snacks for three growing children. During the day, plenty of sunlight came in through the many windows and the French doors that led into the back yard.

Chelsea crouched down to pet the fat tabby that reclined in the corner near the table where they usually ate breakfast and dinner. "Hi, Simba." Her cat yawned and lazily bounced his tail on the tiled floor.

Terrence tapped his hands on the marble countertop and watched as Charisse finished cleaning up from cooking dinner.

He kept much of his firm physique as he edged toward forty years old, and worked out with the same trainer he started in the music business with when he signed his first recording contract twelve years ago.

"How'd it go this weekend?" Charisse asked. One of his celebrity friends who lived in L.A. owned a place on the water in Miami, and he gave Terrence free rein to use it whenever he wanted.

"Good, as usual. Too cold to get *in* the water, but they still had fun when we went out in the boat. You know how Chelsea loves making s'mores, so we did that *every night* in the backyard." He sighed.

Charisse laughed and stuck the last glass in the dishwasher and turned it on. "You know she only demands you do that because you give in. You need to learn how to say no."

"I can't say no to my baby." He sniffed the air. "What's that I smell?"

She placed her hands on her hips. "Don't you have somewhere to be?"

"Not right at this minute."

"You're supposed to be catching a flight to New York for the Grammys." This year he'd been nominated in two categories—Best Rap Performance and Song of the Year.

His dark eyes narrowed. "If I didn't know better, I'd think that you were trying to get rid of me."

"Moi?" Charisse said with mock innocence.

"You made lasagna." Terrence rounded the counter.

"Wait one minute." Charisse spread her arms wide to block his path to the oven.

"No, Daddy. You're going to eat it all and there won't be any left for us," Chelsea said.

Everyone in the family knew how much Terrence loved Charisse's lasagna, to the point where he once jokingly asked her if she was half Italian.

"You've managed to turn my own children against me," he accused her.

"I haven't turned them against you, it's just that everyone knows how greedy you are."

"Yeah, yeah. Where's the lasagna?" He stepped his broad body closer with mock intimidation, looking down at her with eyes filled with humor and his thick, luscious lips curled into a smile.

Goodness, he was handsome! His face was almost perfectly symmetrical, with dark umber skin and a long, narrow nose set in the middle of a face that at one time had been deemed "too pretty" for rap. His wavy black hair had started to gray, but he maintained its dark luster with the diligent application of hair dye. And when he smiled, her heart clenched painfully.

She still remembered the first time she saw him on stage at a small venue where he'd performed with other up-and-coming acts. He wore an earring in each ear and a thick gold chain with a large medallion around his neck. He smiled at her, and she was putty in his palms from that moment on.

"You're really going to do this?" Charisse asked.

"Yes. I'm really going to do this. Don't make me move you." He arched a thick brow.

She cursed him under her breath and stepped aside. Terrence opened the door to the wall oven. Inside sat a warming lasagna, ready for dinner when the kids arrived. He glanced over his shoulder at her and shook his head. "Look at how you treat me. You were going to let me leave and not give me any of this. I can't believe you."

One of the ways they bonded when they first started dating was over their love of food. They'd both enjoyed the adventure of trying new cuisines, especially as the dollars in his bank account expanded. She missed those days.

Terrence rummaged in the drawers and found a metal spatula.

Charisse snatched it away. "Please don't. Let me handle this."

"Are you going to fix me a plate?" he asked.

"Yes, but only because if I don't, you'll scoop out half the lasagna and there won't be enough for me and the kids. Don't forget, they've all inherited your hearty appetite."

Well, the last two, anyway. Ennis was from a previous relationship, and Terrence adopted him after they got married.

She bumped him out of the way with her hip and proceeded to scoop the steaming pasta onto a plate. She added homemade garlic bread and wrapped the entire dish in foil. "There you go. Now, be gone with you."

"Thank you." Terrence took the plate right as his phone rang and he looked at the screen before answering. "Yo, what's up?" He paced away from her. "I just dropped off the kids, and I should be at the airport in about half an hour."

Charisse folded her arms and shook her head at the lie. With the airport at least an hour's drive, the only way he'd make it there in half an hour was through time travel.

"Man, I'm not giving her no message for you."

Charisse walked over and sent him a silent question with her eyes.

"It's Bo," he mouthed.

"Tell him I said hi," she whispered.

He rolled his eyes. "She said to tell you hi." Pause. "He said to tell you hi back and that he hopes you pampered yourself during your break from the kids."

"Thank you, Bo. I enjoyed my weekend off, but of course I'm happy to have my babies back." She spoke loud so that he could hear.

"Happy now?" Terrence asked his friend. There were a few seconds of silence, and then he said, "All right. I'll holler when I land. We can set something up when I get there." Pause. "A'ight. Peace." He hung up the phone and took a deep breath. "My work is never done."

"You're a very important man. I take it he went up early for the pre-Grammy parties?"

"Yeah, he did."

"Good luck tonight."

"Thanks. But it's an honor just to be nominated."

"But even better to win," they finished together and laughed.

Chelsea scampered over and hugged his waist. "Knock 'em dead, Daddy."

"Thanks, princess. I needed that extra boost." He gave her a squeeze, kissed her forehead, and then started out of the kitchen.

"Bye, boys!" he hollered.

Ennis and Junior came out of their rooms.

"Good luck, Pops," Ennis said.

"Yeah, good luck, Dad," Junior added.

"Thanks."

The three dapped and then the boys disappeared again.

Terrence turned at the door. "Think I have a chance?"

Charisse was one of the few people, assuming there were any others, that he admitted his insecurity to. He wanted the Song of the Year award, no matter how much he joked that the honor was simply in being nominated. Sales on his last album dipped lower than expected, as his unique sound—the lyrical stylings of an East Coast flow combined with the bounce of Southern hip-hop—was replaced by new and younger artists coming onto the scene. His income hadn't declined, though. He expanded his fortune by investing in multiple business ventures—flavored water, a line of specialty vodkas, shoes, and other opportunities presented to him. He courted the idea of retiring, though he wanted to tour one more time before he left the rap game.

"I think you have every chance of winning. Win or lose, you did an amazing job, but I really think you can win, Terrence." She crossed her fingers and held them up. "I have my fingers crossed for you."

His eyes softened on her. "Okay if I call you after the show?"

"Of course. You know you always can."

"Thanks, sweetheart." He gave her the quickest, faintest peck on the cheek. "You're the best." He winked and then left.

Charisse quietly closed the door behind him and stood there for a moment, chest heavy with an emptiness she couldn't seem to shake. His cologne lingered in the entryway. He'd worn the same scent for a long time—a French brand that layered the crispness of citrus over the fullness of musk.

She placed a hand over the spot that he kissed. She shouldn't dwell on the sensation but couldn't help it. Divorced five years, they were in a good place now. They really were, considering how painfully their marriage ended. It took a while to get to this point of being friends and co-parenting in a positive way. But there were times when he touched her that the memories came barreling back and she longed for a simpler time, when they lived in a two-bedroom apartment on the west end and his popularity was limited to a small fan base. Before the record deal, the money, the glamour. Before the many women who'd catch his eye.

"Mom?"

She swung around and faced her eldest son. "Yes, baby?"

"Can we eat now? I'm starving." Ennis's caramel-toned skin was a mixture of his biological father's fairer complexion and her deep brown complexion.

She walked over to him and looped an arm through his. "Yes, we can eat now."

So her marriage was over, but she had three beautiful kids and lived a full life, simply because of them.

## ❧ 2 ❧

Terrence shouldered his way through the crowd at Madison Square Garden, clutching the gold-plated gramophone that proclaimed he won for Song of the Year. As he moved through the producers, musicians, and songwriters, he accepted words of praise, offered his own, and shook hands with more people than he could count.

Bo, his longtime assistant and friend, was somewhere nearby, but he didn't bother to look for him after the backstage interviews. His only concern was to find a quiet corner to call Charisse. Finally, he found a spot at the end of a less-crowded hall that led off the main floor of the venue and dialed her number.

"Hello?" She answered on the first ring, as if she'd been waiting by the phone for his call.

"I won! Did you see?"

"Yes! Terrence, I'm so happy for you. I swear, there's nothing you can't do." Her voice, full of happiness for him, sent chills over his skin.

That was Charisse, his greatest encourager. She'd been that way from day one, even when he doubted himself. Her words kept him hustling at the clubs and opening for better-known acts. He wished she'd been here with him, like in the past, blowing him a kiss from the audience. Then he could squeeze her tight in a celebratory embrace afterward. Instead, he settled for her voice and imagined the grin coming through loud and clear.

"Have you called Grandma Esther yet?" she asked.

"Nah, you were the first person I called. She's probably asleep, anyway. She doesn't stay up like she used to."

His grandmother raised him from the age of twelve, after his father walked out and his mother overdosed on drugs. Those first few years he gave her hell, and as an adult often did things that most definitely didn't make her proud. Yet her love for him never wavered, remaining steadfast no matter how much he screwed up. If Charisse was his encourager, Grandma Esther was his rock.

"Yo T, you coming or what?"

Terrence twisted around to see Bo standing down the hallway. He was a big dude and looked like a light-skinned Terry Crews—with bulging muscles and a bald head. Two lovely young women were with him. Clearly, Bo was in a celebratory mood, too.

"Was that Bo?" Charisse asked.

He turned his back to his friend. "Yeah, but his ass can wait."

Charisse laughed. "You better go. I'm sure you want to do some more networking, and it's time for *me* to go to bed like Grandma Esther."

His mind skated away from the thought of her in bed wearing a thin nightshirt or one of those skimpy nighties that barely covered her bottom and showed off her full breasts to perfection. Some days he couldn't escape the memories. Some days he wanted inside her so bad, his dick hurt.

Though he missed the pre-Grammy events, Terrence was going to the NARAS post-awards party to catch up with friends and do some networking. If he could have his way, he'd head home to Charisse, or she'd come out to the club with him. Back in the day, they used to hit the clubs and stay until the wee hours of the morning. She loved to dance and didn't mind getting raunchy, grinding her ass against him and slow-dancing to an up-tempo beat, in their own world and simply enjoying each other.

Later, if they managed to control themselves until they arrived at the hotel, they'd screw until exhausted. Though there were times they never made it that far and suffered through the discomfort of a back-seat hook up, her dress pushed up and his hands gripping her hips. He'd lick the sweat that made her dark skin glimmer and force her to hold his gaze as she rode him into ecstasy. Those days were long gone.

"All right, I'll let you go, old woman." He made sure to keep a teasing tone and eliminate the disappointment from his voice. He'd talk to her all night if she let him.

"Hey, I'm not as young as I used to be, and I don't have your energy. Cut me some slack." She giggled and then her voice sobered. "Song of the Year. Now you have two Grammys. How many people can say that? I'm so proud of you, Terrence."

His chest tightened. This woman really knew how to get to him.

"Thanks. Once NARAS sends the official award to management with my name on it, I'll bring it by next time I come over so you and the kids can see it."

"Why bother? You seen one Grammy, you've seen them all," Charisse said airily.

Terrence laughed. "I'm bringing it anyway, and you're gonna love it."

He glanced back at Bo, who stood with his arms crossed, legs spread apart. He raised his eyebrows at Terrence.

"I better go. Bo looks like he wants to fire me even though I'm his boss."

"Isn't that the way it's always been? He has to keep you in line. Have fun and stay out of trouble. Good night, T-Murder," she said softly.

Terrence closed his eyes and absorbed the sweetness of her voice. He firmed his lips as regret soured in his chest. If only he could turn back the clock, he'd do so many things differently.

"Good night, sweetheart." He disconnected the call and stared at the blank screen for several seconds. Then he took a deep breath and trudged toward his friend with extra swagger in his walk. He stepped over to where one of the women—amber-skinned with curly blonde locks and gray eyes that looked seductively into his— stood waiting. He recognized her as one of the performers' backup dancers. She looked about twenty-four, the same age Charisse had been when he married her.

"Never seen one of those. Can I touch it?" the woman asked.

"I don't even know your name," he said.

She blushed shyly. "Kimberly, but I go by Kim."

"Well Kim, you can touch it—if you give me a kiss on the cheek first."

She blushed again but obliged, pressing soft lips against his jaw. She smelled good, and his male brain shifted gears and paid closer attention. She was perfect. She looked nothing like Charisse, who had dark skin, dark eyes, and thick coily hair she ran to the hairdresser to straighten every two to three months.

Maybe he'd take Kim home tonight. Maybe not. He'd see how the evening unfolded.

He handed her the award and her eyes widened. "It's heavier than I expected. Is it real gold?"

"Gold plated," Terrence replied.

"Can we go now?" Bo asked.

"Go ahead, man, you lead the way."

"That's what I'm talking 'bout."

Bo took off with the other woman and Terrence flung an arm around Kim's shoulders and pulled up the rear.

"What are you doing after the party?" he asked.

She glanced up at him with a coquettish smile. "Whatever you're doing." Not so shy after all.

"I don't know if you can hang with us. We go hard," he warned. The NARAS party was not the place to cut loose, but he and Bo would definitely hit a club or two afterward. They'd get drunk off top-shelf liquor, and if they were lucky, get high on some good weed.

"I may surprise you. Maybe I don't know if you can hang with me."

Well, damn.

Terrence grinned, certain she'd help him forget the woman he really wanted to be with tonight. The woman he met fourteen years ago, married two years later, and who changed his life. The woman whose name he tattooed over his heart on their four-year anniversary to prove his love after too many fuck ups—and never removed it, even after they split.

Yeah, Kim should help him forget Charisse.

At least, he hoped so. If only for a few hours.

$\mathcal{H}$ 3 $\mathcal{H}$

errence and Bo sat in a booth at Darn Good, a locally owned restaurant off Candler Road in existence for over thirty years. The menu hadn't changed in all that time. From the outside, the place looked like a hole in the wall, but they served delicious meals—simple but hearty breakfasts and simple but hearty lunches that consisted of one meat and two vegetables. Terrence had been coming here for years, and he and the owner, Miss Margaret, were good friends. In the early days when cash was low, he could always stop by and Miss Margaret would fill his arms with leftovers so he could feed his wife and adopted son. In appreciation of her kindness, he shouted out Darn Good in a couple of songs when he became famous. The free publicity made the little restaurant popular and its owner a minor celebrity.

Stopping in from time to time did more than feed his belly. The visits satisfied his appetite for nostalgia and reminded him of where he came from. Still bleary-eyed after flying back from New York after a promotional gig and time spent in the studio doing a feature for one of the record company's popular R&B artists, he and Bo remained inconspicuous in thick jackets and skull caps pulled low on their foreheads.

Terrence checked messages on his phone while Bo wolfed down grits with sugar sprinkled on them—full-on blasphemy in a place like this—and shoveled eggs and toast into his mouth. When he finally took a break, he asked, "What are you working on?"

"I asked Kamisha to check on vacation spots for this summer's trip," Terrence said, referring to his other assistant. Kamisha handled travel arrangements, organized his calendar, and worked from the office. Bo was a jack-of-all-trades who traveled with him and acted as a go-between for any and all issues he didn't want to address directly.

"You taking Charisse and the kids on a trip this summer, too?"

He glanced up at his friend, who studied him from across the table. "Yes."

Bo knew the answer to the question before he asked. Terrence and Charisse had been divorced for five years, but the past two summers, he took her and the kids on a two-week vacation and made it plain that would be their annual ritual for years to come. This year he was thinking about the Galapagos Islands, since Charisse and Ennis liked to snorkel.

Of course, he knew why Bo asked. He thought it was weird Terrence vacationed with his ex.

Bo wiped his mouth and dropped the crumpled napkin on the table. "Yo, I still don't get it. I think Charisse is a sweetheart, and God knows she put up with a lot of shit from your ass, but she's your *ex*."

Terrence sighed and set down the phone. "What's the big deal? She's the mother of my children, and we're still friends. We get along. There's nothing wrong with us spending time together with the kids. It's good for them to see us getting along."

Bo eyed him skeptically. "So the only reason you plan these vacations is to present a united front for the kids?"

That wasn't the only reason he arranged these trips. During those two weeks, he experienced their family life again, as if they weren't divorced and living apart. They ate together, went sight-seeing, and because they were five people with five different opinions, they argued about what they wanted to do from day to day. And he loved every minute of it.

He also loved to watch his ex. She was a darn good mother who played with the kids, kissing on them even in the middle of an intense water volleyball match. Half the time he didn't join in. Under the pretense of working, he sat on the side of the private pool and watched behind dark sunglasses. *Watched Charisse.* She was beautiful and sexy in a one-piece bathing suit that she thought was more modest but made his imagination run wild.

Charisse still turned him on, and if she turned him on, she turned on other men—which he could barely stand to think about. Thank goodness she kept her relationships low-key. In all these years he'd never actually seen her with another man. He liked to think there was no one else, because he couldn't tolerate the thought of another man touching her. Quite ironic, considering his track record. Before the blow up that ended their marriage, he never flaunted his extramarital hookups, but there had been plenty of questionable photos, rumor, and innuendo—some true, some false—and she'd have to be blind and deaf not to know what he'd been up to.

"Of course I'm organizing these vacations for the kids," Terrence said.

"Come on, dawg, it's me."

Terrence chuckled. "I'm serious."

Bo drummed thick fingers on the table as Terrence resumed scrolling through emails, pretending not to notice.

"I think it's great you and Charisse have such a solid relationship, but how do you think your new woman is going to handle the fact that you're vacationing with your ex?"

Terrence continued scrolling. "I don't have a new woman."

"When you do, you think she's gon' like you hanging out on the beach or whatever with your ex-wife? Any woman with half a brain would be threatened by that. Come on, man, you're looking for trouble."

Terrence put down the phone and glared at Bo. He firmed his

voice to make it clear the conversation should come to an end. "My ex-wife and my kids are part of my life. Whoever enters my life now will simply have to deal."

"And the shorty from the Grammys? You been seeing her for a couple of weeks now."

He didn't normally take the number of one-night stands, but he'd liked Kim and flew her out to see him a few times. He didn't know where this relationship was going, but for now she filled a void.

"Like I said, she'll have to deal. If she has a problem with Charisse, that's her problem. She can simply move on. We ain't in love."

"Cool, cool." Bo nodded his head. "I just wanted to check, man. I'd hate to see anyone get hurt."

"Ain't nobody getting hurt. Kim's grown. I'm grown. We're having fun, that's all." Terrence tucked the phone into his pocket. "I'm going to take a leak. Finish your food and when I get back, let's bounce. We have a meeting at eleven and I don't want to be late."

"A'ight man."

Terrence slid from the booth and walked toward the restrooms in the back of the restaurant.

Bo and Grandma Esther were the only two people to warn him that he should change his ways or risk losing his wife. He didn't listen to either of them. He listened to his own lust and the people who encouraged the bad behavior. And quite frankly, he enjoyed himself.

His penis hadn't been the only thing getting stroked during that period. His oversized ego had been, too. Being a celebrity was a drug all its own, and so was having women fawn all over you— screaming your name, slipping you their number, and willing to do anything for a night in your arms.

Those days used to be fun, but he didn't go out as much as he used to anymore. Most nights he stayed his ass at home. He figured out too late there was nothing out there for him.

## ❧ 4 ❧

Charisse examined her reflection in the gold standing mirror in a corner of her bedroom. Her daughter, Chelsea, sat cross-legged on the high four-poster bed watching her primp and prepare for her date with Austin, a marketing consultant she met at the grocery store, of all places.

They'd been seeing each other for over a month, and she liked him a lot. He was polite and funny, and they definitely had some chemistry. Sure, it wasn't the explosive chemistry she used to have with Terrence, but none of the men she dated since they split managed to curl her toes and make her heart race the way her ex-husband did. She learned to accept that and enjoy their company nonetheless.

She turned and faced her daughter and placed her hands on her hips. "How do I look?"

"Pretty."

"You're not saying that because I'm your mother?"

Chelsea shook her head vigorously, her braids swinging around her head. "You look very pretty, Mommy. You always look pretty."

"And you are my little angel."

"Princess," Chelsea corrected.

"Oh yes, how could I forget. My princess."

Charisse took one more look at her reflection. She liked dressing up, and tonight she looked sexy in an electric-blue dress, gold pumps, and heavy makeup that contoured her cheeks and elongated her lashes.

"All right, let's go. Grandma will be here any minute, and then I need to leave."

Because she planned to stay out the entire night, she asked her mother to sleep over. She hadn't shared her decision to spend the night with Austin, in case she changed her mind over the course of the evening. They'd made love before, but she never spent the night, though he made it clear she was welcome to do so.

Normally, Ennis watched his younger siblings when she went out, but since she would be gone overnight, she wanted an adult in the house.

She grabbed her purse and she and Chelsea exited the bedroom. Down the hall, she rapped twice on her eldest son's door and poked her head in. He and Junior sat on the floor, staring up at the TV screen, playing a video game.

"I'm on my way out. You guys be good."

"Bye, Mom," Junior said over his shoulder without taking his gaze from the screen.

Ennis glanced back and did a double take. "Wow, you look pretty, Mom."

"Thank you, honey."

As she and Chelsea walked down the hallway, she heard the front door open. "Mom, is that you?"

"It's me," her mother called back.

Chelsea ran ahead and as Martha came into view, flung herself into her grandmother's arms. "Grandma, doesn't Mommy look pretty?"

Her mother wore an auburn wig and looked relaxed in a pair of dark jeans and tennis shoes. The lines at the corners of her eyes crinkled when she nodded and grinned. "Very pretty. I think you're in for a really good night tonight," she said with a wink.

"And I appreciate you doing this for me." Her mother encouraged her to date again after she and Terrence initially split. It took a year to get back on the dating scene, but as the saying goes, the best way to get over someone was to get under a new someone. Once she started spending time with other men, the loneliness didn't hit as hard and she didn't have much time to feel sorry for herself.

"I'll head out now so I'm not late. I'll see you guys tomorrow. Thanks again, Mom."

"Have fun!" her mother called.

"Name?"

"Ross," Austin answered. "Austin Ross."

Arm in arm, Charisse and Austin stood at the host stand of Notte, a large Italian restaurant with an intimate ambiance thanks to the dark wood walls, dimmed lights, and votive candles flickering on each table. Charisse had saved her appetite, and the scent of basil and marinara sauce made her anxious to eat.

"There you are." The host checked off Austin's name. "Follow me, please."

Tonight Austin wore a long-sleeved dress shirt under a blue sweater vest and tie. The glasses on his face gave him a distinguished look along with the neat, close-cropped hair with gray coming in at the edges above his ears.

He held onto her hand as they followed the host through the maze of tables, but as they were walking, her gaze fell on a face she never expected to see. Terrence snapped a selfie with a couple of fans and then flung an arm around the neck of the young woman by his side. He did it in a negligent way, as if he'd done it many times before.

They looked good together. Terrence in black jeans and a black turtleneck because of the cool March evening, and the young woman pretty in a long-sleeved but short, skintight black dress and the type of killer heels Charisse gave up wearing a few years ago.

She swallowed hard as hurt bloomed in the pit of her stomach. She felt a little sick, the same way she used to feel when Terrence's nameless, faceless girlfriends developed names and faces on Instagram or gossip blogs. It was so much easier when she couldn't see them and could pretend they didn't exist.

Her left hand tightened fractionally around Austin's, and then the host stopped beside a table and waved his hand. "Will this work?" he asked.

"Yes, this works," Austin answered.

But Charisse wasn't paying attention. She kept her eyes trained on Terrence and his latest squeeze, laughing and talking with the patrons. As they were saying goodbye, he saw her, and the smile died on his face. His gaze dropped to where her hand was still enveloped in Austin's.

She smiled and glanced away, allowing Austin to help her into the chair and off her suddenly unsteady feet. The host handed them both menus and promised the waiter would arrive soon.

"You're okay with this table, right?" Austin asked.

Perhaps he thought her silence meant disapproval, but little did he know she had experienced a shock.

"It's perfect," she replied. She looked at the menu.

"Hi, Charisse," a deep voice said to her right.

Tension filled her shoulders. She should have known he would stop by the table, but she hoped that he would leave to avoid a confrontation. With all the dirt he did during their marriage, one thing remained constant, and that was Terrence's jealous streak. She kept her post-marital relationships low-key for that very reason.

He was particularly sensitive about the men who worked in music with him, and whenever they attended industry events, he made sure to stick close, as if worried someone would take her away from him. One time he ended up in a scuffle with another rapper over a song.

"Bomb Pussy" was a raunchy rap Terrence wrote about the pleasure he received from being inside his woman and from performing cunnilingus on her. Everyone knew the song was about Charisse, though he never openly admitted it. When the rapper in question recited the vulgar lyrics backstage at a show while looking right at Charisse, Terrence flew into a rage and swung on him. If it weren't for security, one or both men would have ended up in the hospital.

She used to believe his jealousy proved that he loved her, despite his affairs. God, she'd been so foolish.

"Hi, Terrence."

"Kids at home?" he asked, eyes boring into hers.

"Yes, as a matter of fact they are. My mother's there to make sure they don't burn the house down." She smiled tightly and glanced at the woman with him. She looked uncomfortable, shifting from one leg to the other. Up close she appeared younger than Charisse initially thought. She looked about twenty-four, around fifteen years younger than her ex. So typical.

"This is Kim Jones. Kim, this is my ex-wife, Charisse Burrell." Terrence looked at her date. "Hi, I'm the ex-husband. I'm sure you've heard of me, Terrence T-Murder Burrell."

*Did he place extra emphasis on murder?* She almost rolled her eyes. He acted as if he earned the name from literally murdering people, instead of how he earned it—building a reputation of "murdering" MCs in cypher competitions and street corner rap battles. He was clearly posturing, though she didn't think her date could be intimidated. He was so laid back.

Austin extended his hand. "I'm—"

"Austin," she filled in for him. She didn't want him to give Terrence his full name. She didn't trust him.

A muscle in Terrence's jaw twitched. He didn't shake Austin's hand. "Guess I'll let you finish your meal. We still on for the tour tomorrow?"

Tomorrow they took their eldest on a tour of Morehouse College, one of the schools he considered attending after he graduated next spring. It was not something they needed to discuss right this minute.

"Yes, we're still on for tomorrow," she answered.

"Cool. See you then. Nice to meet you, Austin."

"Likewise."

They left the table and Charisse breathed easier.

"Everything okay?"

Austin's gaze remained trained on the menu.

"Yes, everything is okay." She reached across the table and he put his hand in hers.

She wanted to reassure him. Having an ex-husband who was bigger than life could sometimes be intimidating for other men. Not to mention so many of his songs consisted of boasts about his sexual prowess, tales of growing up poor and black in the hood, and bragging about his money, jewelry, and cars.

At least, those were the ones that received the most radio play. Only diehard fans knew about the songs where he bemoaned the ravages of poverty, encouraged young people to strive for their dreams, and cursed the political powers that be for their negligence and selfishness as they handled government affairs.

Austin squeezed her hand. "Good."

"There's something I want to tell you."

"Okay."

"I have an overnight bag in the car, and the reason my mother is watching the kids tonight is because…I'd like to spend the night with you, if that's okay."

A broad grin spread across his lips. "Of course that's okay. I've missed you since the last time, and when you left like you did, I wasn't sure…"

"I know. With the kids…"

He shook his head. "No need to explain. I understand. But I'm glad you can make time for me tonight." He rubbed a thumb back and forth over her hand.

"Good."

"Good."

They both laughed and she returned her attention to the menu choices, much more upbeat. She would not allow Terrence to kill the mood. Now that her date was back on track, she allowed her mind to dissect what happened and reflected on the past.

Terrence used to always have a perfectly logical explanation for any suspicious-looking photos that popped up online and an excuse for showing up late after engagements. His favorite was to say that he was working in the studio. Another was to say that he was in a meeting that ran over and they went for drinks afterward and lost track of time.

If she found any evidence of his betrayal, he instantly became contrite and apologetic. He would buy her a piece of jewelry or send her on a shopping spree and come home on time for a while. Then after a period, sometimes only a couple of months later, the behavior started all over again.

In the beginning, he used to take her out. They partied together, but that happened less the bigger his star shined. She knew it was so he could hook up with other women, though he insisted that was not the case. And he always brought up the fact that someone needed to keep an eye on the kids, as if they couldn't hire a caretaker or her mother wasn't available.

After a while, she stopped yelling and stopped questioning him. She grew tired of hearing, *These hoes won't leave me alone* or *I don't know where that number came from.* She ignored the signs and pretended she didn't see the numbers or smell the perfume in his clothes. Until the day came when she could no longer ignore, and one of his side chicks, a stripper named Brenda, approached her while she was at the grocery store with her two youngest. Brenda yelled and screamed, accosting her as if *she* were the wife and Charisse the side chick.

Then the photos were plastered online, and a video appeared on TMZ with this woman yelling and tossing boxes of cereal while Charisse's bodyguard held her at bay. Charisse had abandoned her cart and run off with her kids.

It was one thing to deal with the infidelity privately, but the public humiliation had been too much. Terrence's affairs chipped away at her self-esteem, but that public display damaged her pride. The video showed she was a woman on the run. On the run from the truth that she was no longer married.

Terrence claimed he didn't know Brenda. He called her a crazy stalker and said there was nothing going on between them. But when Brenda posted a sonogram of their alleged unborn child on Instagram, that was the death knell of their marriage.

The media hounded Charisse, articles were printed with all sorts of tacky headlines about whether or not she could satisfy a man like T-Murder, and both she and the other woman's images sat next to each other while people on social media made hurtful, unfair comparisons between them. One in particular crushed her spirits. *I'm not saying he's right, but I understand,* the person posted.

Terrence finally admitted to having sex with Brenda but swore he used protection—as if that made the betrayal okay. Charisse filed for divorce. When the young woman retracted her statement —she wasn't pregnant after all—and admitted she'd wanted to hurt Terrence the way he hurt her by dismissing their affair as nothing, Charisse plowed on.

Their marriage was broken. She was broken. She simply couldn't stand to be with him anymore.

In the end, he was generous with support. He bought the house she wanted and gave her everything she asked for and more, claiming he did so because taking care of their kids was a full-time job. Making sure they ate well, checking their homework, getting them to school on time, and being an emotional support system for them while he was on the road was all valuable and worthy of decent pay. In reality, she suspected his generosity sprang from guilt, maybe shame, or a combination of the two.

It took them over two years to arrive at a place where they could actually be friendly and not cold to each other. After tonight, she wondered if that long-standing truce had somehow been broken.

## ❦  5  ❧

"It's nice here," Terrence said to his grandmother over the phone as he walked the Morehouse College campus.

"How many schools have you visited so far?"

"This is the third one, but it's my favorite."

"You're not the one going to college, dear heart."

"I know. But if I were, I'd pick Morehouse."

The staff arranged a private tour of the campus, which Terrence appreciated. As Charisse and Ennis strolled ahead of him with one of the school's student ambassadors, he took stock of the students trudging to class, others laughing in groups, and the old buildings within whose walls young minds were being prepared for life in the "real world."

He never attended college himself, but taking these trips with his son to visit the campuses made him think about what his life could have been like if he'd had the opportunity. He made a lot of money and took care of the people he loved, evidence that a college education was not the only way to be successful, but he couldn't help but wonder what his day-to-day would look like if he'd gone to college.

Especially a place like this, founded in 1867 to educate young black men otherwise shut out of the country's institutions of higher learning. The first sentence of their mission statement alone impressed him. *The mission of Morehouse College is to develop men with disciplined minds who will lead lives of leadership and service.*

At least he could give his kid the opportunity to get a higher education. Being able to live vicariously through Ennis made him proud that he could provide this opportunity for all his kids. His son might attend one of the top HBCUs in the country, which graduated some of the most successful black academics and professionals. Famous alumni who'd attended included Dr. Martin Luther King, Jr., Samuel L. Jackson, Spike Lee, and former Atlanta mayor Maynard Jackson. And maybe, one day, they would add Ennis Burrell to that list.

"It's never too late to get an education. Adults go back to school all the time. Don't rule it out, dear heart," Grandma Esther said.

He smiled at her encouraging words. She never put limitations on his dreams, and for that he was thankful. "I'll think about it. Who knows, maybe I'll take a class or two—see how it feels. Anyway, I gotta go soon. We're almost at the admissions building. How are you feeling?"

She had a stroke a few weeks ago but was back at home with a full-time caretaker, which she resented but Terrence would not take no for an answer.

"I'm fine. You worry too much."

"There's no such thing as worrying too much. You're not giving Dana any more trouble, are you?"

"No, I'm not. That girl has a strong constitution. I thought she'd quit by now, but she's still here. She done wore me out. I'm plum tired being a you-know-what to her and she still here, just smiling and being patient and friendly. You must be paying her real nice."

Terrence chuckled. "She's used to ornery people like you. I'ma come see you next week, a'ight?"

She lived in Macon, where she raised him, and lived in the same house his grandfather purchased for her decades ago.

"All right, dear heart. Give my love to Ennis and Charisse. You take care."

"You, too."

Terrence hung up and focused on the three people ahead of him. While he enjoyed the tour of the campus, one thing did mar the experience. He and Charisse had barely spoken since they met up. She spoke to Ennis and the tour guide, he spoke to Ennis and the tour guide, but they said maybe five words to each other. He was still smarting from when he saw her last night with that Austin dude and wondered whether or not she'd slept with him.

She wore her hair in the same style she did then—straight and filled out with strategically placed tracks, letting it touch her shoulders, every now and again blowing around her face when a light breeze swept across the campus. She wore a silk blouse with three-quarter-length sleeves and jeans that hugged her beautiful derrière, making it hard to keep his eyes off her. Charisse had always been a sexy woman without even trying. When he saw her last night, though, she'd been trying. She looked hella good, and he didn't doubt for one second that dude tried to get in her panties.

Did she let him?

He ground his teeth. He needed to know if they slept together. It was eating him alive.

He looked down at his hand and saw that he'd crushed the brochure. He hadn't realized he'd done that and tucked it into his back pocket.

They came to a stop at the admissions building and the guide said, "This is the end of the line for me. I hope you enjoyed your tour. Do you have any more questions?"

"I'm good. Mom, Pops?"

"I don't have any questions," Charisse said.

Terrence shook his head, indicating he didn't have any, either.

"All right then. I'll walk you into the office, and the admissions counselor will then have a few words with you. I hope you do decide to attend Morehouse. I think you'll love it."

The young man led them inside to a hallway and then a couple doors down to one of the offices. They were greeted by an older woman wearing glasses.

"Welcome back!" she said in a booming but friendly voice. "I'm sure Stephen did a great job with the tour, but I'm here to answer any additional questions that you may have. Thank you, dear." Stephen nodded and left them alone. "Let me know your concerns, but by no means is this the last chance you have to talk to us. We want to keep in touch with you after today so that if you have additional questions, we can answer them. We also want to share information with you about activities taking place on campus that Ennis might be interested in attending." She punctuated her little speech with a smile.

"Stephen mentioned there was additional literature I could take a look at," Ennis said.

"Absolutely! And I'll have you fill out a sign-up sheet so we can add you to our activities mailing list."

"Sounds good." Ennis glanced at both of his parents for permission.

"You go ahead and we'll wait out here," Charisse said.

"All right, we'll only take a few minutes and we'll be right back." With a hand at his back, the woman guided Ennis into a back office. Terrence and Charisse sat down in the empty chairs, leaving one empty chair between them.

She crossed her legs away from him and perused one of the brochures. A young man, who didn't look much older than Ennis, stood at the counter leafing through a magazine. In the back, the muted sounds of other staff having conversations could be heard.

"How was your date last night?" Terrence asked.

She didn't look at him. "It went well. How was yours?"

"Good." Liar.

He didn't sleep a wink and his penis turned into a wet noodle, unable to stand erect so he could have sex with Kim. All because his imagination tortured him with thoughts of Charisse screwing another man. She looked so sexy with red lips, sultry eyes, and that blue dress hugging her shapely body. He'd wanted her so badly he almost upended the restaurant table and dragged her back to his place to fuck her good and long and remind her who she used to belong to.

Today, those tight jeans made his imagination run wild all over again. He used to have the right to touch her. Now he practically sat on his hands like a good little boy while his penis grew hard in the admissions office of Morehouse College.

He glanced over at her. "You haven't said much today."

"Neither have you." She looked up at him.

"Been seeing that guy long?"

She shrugged. "Not long."

"How long is not long?"

She sighed. "About a month, Terrence."

"You screwing him?"

Her eyes opened wide. "What?"

"It's okay if you are," he said, his body growing tense.

"I know it is, but I don't think it's any of your business who I'm screwing."

"So you *are* screwing him?" He felt as if someone dropped a cinder block on his chest.

She glanced at the young man at the counter and lowered her voice. "It's none of your business. You were with someone, too, and you don't see me asking you about her."

He laughed shortly, bitterly. "You've never asked me about any…"

Pain flashed in her eyes and she turned away from him, folding her arms across her stomach.

*Shit.*

"I'm sorry." He lifted a hand to reach for her, but let it drop. She wouldn't want him to touch her right now, of that he was certain. "I just didn't know you were out there like that, you know?" He'd assumed she was always alone. Had hoped that was the case.

"Out there like what?" She faced him with a glare. "You're not the only one who has needs."

The words hung in the air between them, and Terrence saw red. Some primal, savage force in him raised its ugly head, and he gripped the armrest.

Charisse swung her head away from him again while his fingers tightened over the piece of metal. He released, then curled his fingers over the cool steel, and released again. He did that multiple times before the action was no longer sufficient to control the surge of energy coursing through his body.

He bolted from the chair and left the office. Out in the hallway, he nodded at a student and then walked down the hall, all the way to the opposite end of where they'd come in. A burning need to scream overcame him, but how crazy would he look screaming in the middle of the building like a crazy person. He wanted to smash everything in sight.

*You're not the only one who has needs.*

Through a window in the double doors, he watched the young people walking around on campus. He was breathing hard.

"Calm down. Calm down."

He couldn't stand the thought of another man making her wet. Driving into her. Loving on her chocolate nipples. Squeezing her bottom and licking her soft skin. Burying his face between her thighs. Tasting the sweet dampness of her clit. He was enraged. That shit also hurt like hell and gave him a fractional taste of the pain he must have inflicted on her with his cheating over the years. Was this how she'd felt? He couldn't handle it. It felt as if someone had tied a noose around his neck and was slowly tightening it and cutting off his oxygen.

He forced his way back into the office, and the door slammed against the wall. Charisse jumped and the young man behind the counter looked up from his magazine.

Terrence marched over to her, slammed his hands on the chair's armrests, and brought his face down to hers. "Don't you ever bring him into my fucking house."

He straightened and pushed his way back out the door.

## ❧ 6 ❧

Terrence stood with his back against the Range Rover, arms crossed and feet crossed at the ankles. He was in front of the garage at the house talking to Ennis, who wanted to discuss his options for college. Charisse went shopping and would pick up the two younger kids from a birthday party and bring them home later.

Ennis stood facing his father, hands shoved into the pockets of his baggy jeans. "It's so hard to decide. I can't make up my mind at all."

"You don't have to decide right now. You still have time. Figure out what's a must-have at any school that you attend. Then make a list of your top schools. Check out the pros and cons of attending each one, and narrow your list to the ones that tick the most boxes from your list of must-haves."

Ennis nodded his understanding. "Honestly, if I needed to choose now, I'd say Morehouse. But then that means staying in Atlanta, and I don't know if I want to do that. I kind of feel like I need to be on my own and have a chance to grow up a little." He ventured a look at his father, as if nervous about what he thought of the desire to move away.

"I feel you. You can do that here in Atlanta, though. Remember during the tour Stephen said you'll have to live on campus. You won't have your mom all up in your business, if that's what you're worried about."

"Definitely that part." Ennis laughed.

"Listen, you know you don't have to start school right away, right? You could take some time off. What do people call it nowadays...a gap year? Take a break and experience life outside of school, take that time to find yourself and figure out what you want to do. You could work, travel, do whatever you want."

"You guys would let me do that?" Ennis asked with a wrinkled brow.

"I haven't talked to your mom about it, but I don't see why not. This is your life. You gotta live it—not me, not your mom, you feel me? You gotta live with the choices you make. If you don't think you're ready for college, take a break and figure things out."

"I want to make the right choices," Ennis said, still looking uncertain.

"You will. I have confidence in you. But even if you don't, what do you think is gonna happen? You think you gonna die?"

Ennis laughed. "No."

"A'ight then. Here's something I learned a long time ago. There's value in failure. Remember when you had that bike and you came up with the brilliant idea to build your own ramp and do stunts cause you saw some idiot on YouTube doing the same thing? I told you to wait and let me hire a professional to build a sturdy one for you. Remember that?"

"I remember," Ennis replied with an embarrassed smile.

"And what happened?"

"The ramp didn't hold up and I busted my ass."

"You busted your ass, like I told you would happen. But you learned a valuable lesson, didn't you? You learned to be patient and not risk your safety like that again."

"Yeah."

"That's what I mean. Failing is not the end of the world. That's how we learn, okay?"

"Okay."

Terrence yawned and rubbed his belly. "I'ma head home. Make your list and call me later if you want to talk some more."

"All right. Thanks, Pops." They bumped fists and Ennis sauntered toward the house.

Terrence pushed off the grill of the car but suddenly had an idea. "Ennis," he said, motioning with a hand for his son to come closer.

Ennis ambled back over to him.

"How's your mom doing?" Terrence asked.

"What do you mean?"

He shrugged, trying to remain nonchalant. "She got a boyfriend that you know of?"

Ennis laughed. "Mom? No. I mean...well, she dates. She's never introduced us to anyone, so I figure it's never serious."

"So she's always dated?"

Ennis shrugged. "I guess." He was clamming up, perhaps feeling like he was betraying her, but Terrence needed to know more.

"You ever hear her mention a guy named Austin?"

He shouldn't bring him up, but Austin bothered him. Not only because seeing him was the first time he saw his ex-wife with another man, but because Austin represented everything Terrence was not. He looked like the kind of man Charisse deserved. Kind, thoughtful, respectful. He'd treat her like the queen she was, something Terrence had failed miserably at.

"Maybe once or twice. I think that's the guy she went out with last night, but I don't really pay that close attention, to be honest." Ennis paused and looked back at the house, as if making sure no one was listening, but no one else was in the house right now. "I probably shouldn't tell you this, but...sometimes I think she misses you."

"What makes you say that?" Terrence held his breath.

Ennis shrugged. "She gets kinda quiet sometimes, after you leave, as if she's thinking or something. You know?"

"Yeah, I know." He knew all too well. "Thanks."

Ennis scuffed the bottom of his shoe against the driveway.

"You want to say something else?" Terrence asked.

Ennis looked up at him. "You trying to get back with her?"

"That's grown folks' business."

"I'm asking cause…well, she cried a lot when you guys divorced."

Terrence rubbed the back of his head, guilt filling his chest. "That was all me. I didn't realize what I had at the time." He had never discussed the breakup in any detail with his son, but he was certain Ennis knew about his infidelities. It wasn't the kind of thing you could keep a secret or keep from children when the dirt was all over social media and the various gossip blogs.

"Now do you realize what you had?" The underlying question being, *If you get back together, are you going to treat her right?*

He nodded. "If I could turn back the clock and fix everything, I would. I failed at marriage, big time, but if I ever get the chance to be with your mom again, I definitely won't screw it up."

Ennis puffed out a breath and stuck his hands in his pockets again. Neither of them spoke for a while. Then he quietly asked, "You think you'll get a chance to be with her again?"

Not with Dudley Do Right in the picture, but Terrence didn't say that out loud. "Maybe. I'll see what the future holds. Go on inside. Make your list like I told you."

"All right. Later."

Terrence climbed into the SUV and watched Ennis go in the front door. His son had given him valuable information, assuming his interpretation of his mother's behavior was correct. Maybe she wasn't involved in a serious relationship with Austin after all.

He didn't want to get his hopes up, but if she still harbored feelings for him, he might have a chance at winning her back.

BEING IN THE STUDIO WAS USUALLY AN ESCAPE FOR TERRENCE, BUT

today was not one of those days. Everyone was upset with him—the producer, the engineer, the assistant engineer, and even the intern, who he snapped at when he brought a sandwich with mayonnaise and Terrence specifically asked for mustard.

They'd all gone on break after a heated exchange because of Terrence's lackluster performance in the booth on his latest project, *Annihilation*. The only person who remained was Bo, who eyed him from one of the leather couches through a haze of weed smoke.

His friend took a drag of the blunt and extended it to Terrence. Terrence shook his head and paced the floor.

"What's going on with you? You're not yourself. You've barely done any work on this album so far, and everything you have done is garbage," Bo said.

Terrence could always count on his unfiltered comments.

*Annihilation* was turning out to be a bust. It's possible he was trying to put out another album too soon after the last one, but he believed he had more stories to tell. He considered the *Hustle* album, his first, his greatest collection of work to date. That single word meant he was ready to take on the world and do whatever it took to succeed. Even the album cover, a simple photo of his back with the word "Hustle" on his shirt, represented the rawness and simplicity of all the tracks.

*Annihilation* should elevate his game and was a surprise for fans, yet the record company breathed down his neck, probably because they suspected he was near the point where he would retire soon. His business ventures netted him millions, and he'd dipped his toe into the acting pool with a few roles on TV and in film, most recently playing himself in an action flick. He couldn't blame the company for wanting to capitalize on his celebrity status before he retired from hip-hop.

"I can't concentrate tonight. I have a lot on my mind." He ran a hand over the back of his head.

"What's going on?"

Should he share? Bo was his closest friend. If he couldn't share with him, who could he share with?

"Charisse is seeing someone."

Bo's eyebrows inched higher. "Word?"

"Some Dudley-Do-Right-looking dude." He rested his back against the wall.

Silence settled in the room as Bo continued to smoke. He let his hand fall between his knees. "It's been five years, man. Did you think she was at home with the kids baking cookies and watching reruns of *Leave it to Beaver* or some shit?" He squinted at Terrence through a screen of smoke.

"Maybe."

They both chuckled, releasing the tension in the room.

"I know it's crazy, but...I guess I still consider her my wife." He swallowed. The truth hurt. He wanted to hold onto her but didn't know how.

"I hear you. So she's your wife, sitting at home with the kids. Doing whatever wives do, holding you down. Except—real talk—you ain't been her husband in a while, dawg. You weren't her husband even when ya'll was married."

Terrence wanted to punch him. Sometimes he hated Bo's unfiltered comments.

But his boy was right, and he wanted Charisse back. So how should he proceed?

## ❧ 7 ❧

"Hello?" The phone woke Charisse up in the middle of the night, and Terrence was on the other end.

"Hey," he said.

"Hey. Is something wrong?" She hadn't heard from him since they took the trip to Morehouse a week ago.

"Not really. Could you come to the door?"

He had a key but never used it.

"Um…"

"I only want to talk."

She pushed down a sigh. "Be right there."

Charisse hung up and lifted her robe from the top of the trunk at the foot of the bed and put it on. She didn't bother to remove the silk scarf from her head. Her ex had seen her look worse.

She padded in slippers down the hall to the front door and opened it. Terrence walked in without a word and she closed the door. They stood on opposite sides of the hall, each with their backs against the wall. He looked at her in that Terrence way he did. He only moved his eyes, letting them wander over her body in a knowing way, and she suddenly regretted meeting with him wearing only panties and a thin camisole beneath the robe.

He licked his bottom lip and then bit into it, and her nipples throbbed. She averted her eyes so he wouldn't see his effect on her. If she could control her body, seeing him wouldn't be nearly as hard.

"Anybody here with you?" he asked.

She frowned. "The kids—"

"Anybody else?"

She sighed. He was obviously still obsessed with the fact that she was seeing someone. "No. No one has ever spent the night here."

He inhaled and exhaled deeply, clearly relieved to hear that bit of news.

"You came all the way out here to ask me if I have company?"

"No, that's not why I came. I came out here because I want to talk about us."

She opened her mouth to speak, but he cut her off with a raised hand.

"I've been thinking about us and the past. I know you don't have any reason to forgive me, and I'm really not asking for forgiveness right now. All I'm doing is asking for a chance."

Charisse pulled the robe tighter and wrapped her arms around her waist. "Where is this coming from? Is this because you saw me with Austin the other night?"

"Yes and no. I've been feeling this way for a long time and been thinking about how I could convince you that I'm different. I came to bare my soul to you. The truth is, I've never stopped loving you. I know I messed up, but if you give me another chance, I'll make it up to you."

He sounded so sincere, and if she hadn't heard similar words dozens, possibly hundreds, of times before, she might fall for them.

"Terrence, there is no point to this conversation. I wasn't enough for you before, and I won't be enough for you now."

"That's not true," he said swiftly. "You're all I need. I don't need anyone else."

She wanted to believe him so much, but she knew the truth.

The scars of his betrayal crisscrossed her heart to make sure she never forgot how he treated her.

"Why now? You haven't tried in five years."

"I didn't want to harass you because you left me. You didn't want me anymore."

"That's not my fault."

"I'm not blaming you. I'm saying...I know why, and I want you to know what you mean to me. I don't want to hold my feelings inside anymore. That's all."

*Don't fall for it.*

"Charisse." His dark eyes pleaded with hers and wrenched at her heart. "I swear to you, not a single day goes by that I don't think about you. When I'm not wishing I could hear your voice or see you. You have no idea how many times a day I pick up the phone with the intention of calling you and change my mind because I don't want to bug you. All the time. All. The. Time. I thought being without you would get easier, but it hasn't."

Charisse bit her bottom lip and stared at the floor. She had to stay strong. He'd been contrite before, but he always went back to his old behavior. "I've moved on with my life. You've moved on with yours. We can't go back now."

"Who says we can't? I know you still care about me."

She looked up at him. "Of course I still care about you. We're friends and we were married and you're the father of my children."

He shook his head vehemently. "Nah, that's not all it is, and you know it. Deep down, you still have feelings for me."

She laughed. "What did I possibly do to make you think that I still have feelings for you?"

"It's not really anything you did." He seemed to hesitate. "One of the kids mentioned they noticed how you act sometimes after I leave. Like you still miss me. Maybe not as much as I miss you, but you miss me."

Anger flared to life inside of her, and Charisse pushed off the wall. "Are you serious right now? You're hitting up our kids for information about me?"

"Calm down."

"What have they told you?"

"I know that you date."

"Of course I date. I'm not a nun." She pointed a finger at him. "I know what this is about. It's about you wanting to have control over me still. You can't and you don't. If I want to see someone, I'll see them, and if I want to stay out all night, I'll stay out all night. I don't have to—"

"Hold up." His brows snapped together and he put up his hands for her to stop talking. "You been staying out all night?"

Charisse clamped her mouth shut. She'd assumed he knew everything. Austin wasn't even the first man she'd spent the night with.

"When I took the kids to Miami in January, were you really hanging with your girlfriends over the weekend, or laying up under some man?"

"Forget I said anything."

"No, no, we're going to lay it all out on the table right now. Who you been spending the night with? You stay the night with old dude that I saw you with at the Italian restaurant?"

Charisse closed her eyes and took a deep breath to wrestle her anger under control. Then she opened her eyes and stared at him. "What I do on my own time is my business."

"You're not gonna answer me?" Terrence asked.

He was breathing hard, the way he did when he held an intense emotion. He could explode at any minute.

He chuckled and shook his head, then stepped away from the wall. "Well, well, well. Dudley Do Right ain't so righteous after all, is he?" The fake smile snapped off his face in an instant. "What's his last name?"

"Enough, Terrence! That was cute when we were dating, but the over-the-top jealousy thing is old and outdated, especially since we're not together anymore."

"Give me his name."

"I'm done. You can show yourself out." She made to walk away, but he slammed his hand against the wall, blocking her path.

"Name."

She looked up at him. They were within millimeters of each other. If she weren't angry, she'd sway into his chest. "What are you doing? Are you drunk?" She sniffed but didn't smell alcohol. Only the stale scent of weed that he probably acquired in the studio.

"I'm not drunk. Tell me his name, Charisse. I deserve to know the name of the man who's screwing my wife. Give me his fucking name."

"First of all, I'm not your wife. Second, do I need to call the police and have them escort you off the premises? Do I need to say that I have a trespasser in the house, someone who's here uninvited?"

He narrowed his eyes at her. "You think you're going to make me leave? This is *my* house. My name is on the deed, too. And I pay the bills here."

He'd done this before when he was angry, and she absolutely hated it. "You think you can control me because you pay the bills? Would it make you happy if I left this house? Why don't you put me out, Terrence?"

He appeared startled by the question.

"Whenever you get mad, this house magically turns into yours. Yes, your name is on the deed, too, but you said it was mine. *I* picked it. I wanted something simple I could manage where the kids and I would be safe from curious fans. I wanted normalcy. But now it's *your* house. Thank you for letting me know where I stand."

"Enough! You know I don't want you to leave, and yes, this is your house. What I want... I just want to talk to the man."

"There is nothing for you to talk to him about."

"I need to know!" he said louder.

"You know everything you need to know! *Go.*"

"Mommy?"

They both swung their heads in the direction of the soft voice. Chelsea stood near the end of the entryway in a nightshirt, and in the dim light Charisse saw the fear etched in her face.

Terrence dropped his arm and Charisse shuffled over to their daughter. She crouched in front of her. "Hey, it's okay. Mommy and Daddy are having a conversation, and our voices got a little loud."

"Everything is okay, princess," Terrence said.

"Go back to bed, and I'll be right there to tuck you in, okay?"

"Can I sleep in your bed tonight?" Chelsea asked.

"Baby, you're too old for that. Remember, we talked about it." On occasion she slipped into Charisse's room in the middle of the night and must've gone in there looking for her and then heard their voices in the hall.

"Please, Mommy."

Charisse sighed, giving in because she wanted the conversation to end and Terrence out of the house. "All right. Only for tonight."

A bright grin covered Chelsea's face now that she'd gotten her way. "Good night, Daddy."

"Good night, princess."

When she was gone, Charisse straightened, and they stared at each other in the silence. She didn't know what else to say to him.

He walked slowly toward her and she stepped back into the wall. He kept coming and placed his hands on either side of her.

"I know I messed us up," he said softly. "I know it's my fault we're not together. It's all on me. But I still love you, and I want to fix it. That's what I came here to tell you in the middle of the night. I left the studio and couldn't wait. You're right, I have no right to be jealous, but the thought of you with this other man is driving me insane. I don't deserve a second chance, but I'm asking for one. I miss you so much. So damn much, sometimes I swear I can't fucking breathe. Tell me what to do. I'll do whatever you want."

Charisse sank her teeth into the inside of her bottom lip. Those words were five years too late. There was no longer anything he could do to save their relationship. It was already dissolved. The one thing she asked him to do was stay away from other women, and he didn't do that. She no longer wanted to risk her heart on him.

Did she miss him? Yes. And despite everything that happened, a piece of her heart did and would always belong to Terrence Burrell. Not because he was the father of her children, but because he was the beautiful man—too pretty for rap—who smiled at her from the stage fourteen years ago and won her heart that very night.

That man had been swallowed up by the industry and no longer existed. The woman she had been no longer existed, either.

"Tell me. What do you want me to do?"

Charisse stared at the beating pulse at the base of his neck because she couldn't look at him. "I want you to go," she said quietly.

He didn't budge, but she heard the sound of his lungs deflate. Then his hands fell away from the wall. He stepped back and stared at her, but she didn't look at him. She dropped her eyes to the floor.

There was nothing left for them to say.

Terrence quietly left without a word.

Charisse wrapped her arms around herself and slid down the wall. A little whimper escaped the back of her throat, and then tears eased from beneath her tightly squeezed lids.

Her body shook as she quietly sobbed and pressed her face to her thighs.

Being strong was so darn hard.

Tuesday morning Charisse chatted on the phone with her mother. The kids were in school and she was at home alone taking care of a few chores. She spent much of the morning walking the property and talking to her yard guy about ideas for sprucing up the lawn and planting flowers near the gazebo or working on a full-scale landscape design project.

Her home was a secluded estate on a multi-acre wooded lot without any neighbors nearby. She loved coming up with new ideas to improve the property, like when she hired contractors to redo the driveway with cobblestone or build a sunroom onto the back.

So far she'd been fortunate with Terrence's generosity, but their relationship had chilled considerably, so she needed to be more judicious about how much she spent on sprucing up the yard. Under normal circumstances, he gave her carte blanche to do whatever she wanted, but this time she'd have to take the money out of her own limited budget and might not be able to spend as much.

Back when they divorced, he promised to always take care of her and said she didn't have to work, but she never completely accepted that idea. He took care of her *now*, but one day he would remarry, and his new wife would not like that he was still taking care of his ex. With that in mind, she took a percentage of the spousal support he gave her every month and turned it over to a financial planner so she'd have retirement income in her old age. She couldn't honestly expect Terrence to finance her lifestyle indefinitely, no matter what he said.

Excited about the work in the yard, she called her mother to run some of her ideas by her. During the course of their conversation, her mother mentioned that a new bachelor moved into the assisted living community where she resided, and he played bridge with them last week. Martha thought he'd been a bit flirtatious with her and considered inviting him to tea one afternoon but was hesitant.

"Mom, you need to go ahead and live your life. Isn't that what you told me after my divorce? Dad's been gone for a while."

She set a bowl of cat food on the floor and Simba trotted over and started eating.

"I know, but he's so classy and refined," her mother said.

Charisse walked into the laundry room. "And what are you, chopped liver? You're pretty, educated, funny, and make a mean tuna casserole. That man would be lucky to have you."

Her mother giggled. "Well, we'll see how everything goes. The group is playing bridge together again on Friday. If he's there, I'll see if I have the same impression that he's interested, and I'll know what to do then."

"I say go for it. Flirt back."

Her mother laughed again. She hoped her mother did take the leap. She lived a fulfilling life with the other seniors at the community, but Charisse suspected she wouldn't mind finding another life partner.

The doorbell chimed.

"That's the cleaning service. Gotta run. Call me Friday night and let me know how bridge went with Mr. Casanova. And you better tell me you asked him to tea, or I'm coming down there to invite him for you."

"You're silly, but I will. I'll ask him."

Charisse dropped the clothes she'd been sorting and went back into the kitchen to check the monitor. The cleaning service used a code to get onto the property, and the maids came once a week to deep clean the house, concentrating on bathrooms and high-traffic common areas like the family room.

She set the phone in the cradle on the counter, but when she looked at the monitor, she didn't see the three women who normally came. Terrence stood on the stoop outside, hands braced on the doorframe, head bowed so she only saw the top of his head.

Should she pretend not to be at home?

After their confrontation, she didn't want to talk to him and did a good job of avoiding him so far. Actually, he avoided her, too.

When he called to speak to the children, she and he didn't talk to each other. The other night, he took them to dinner and a movie. Instead of picking them up like he usually did and coming in to chat for a bit, he sent a car.

If the children noticed the way their parents were behaving, they didn't say a word. She and Terrence would eventually have to sort through this impasse in their own way, but today was not that day.

She hit the intercom button. "Terrence, what do you want? I'm busy right now."

"Charisse, open the door. I need to talk to you. Please."

She didn't want to hear any more of his jealous ranting. "Not today. I have a million things to do, and I'm not in the mood to argue."

He lifted his head and stared straight into the camera's lens. The hollowed-out expression in his eyes startled her.

"Please open the door. I'm trying real hard not to use my key."

Worried by what she saw on the screen, Charisse rushed to the front door and swung it open. She stared at her ex. His eyes were red and damp around the edges. He'd obviously been crying.

"What's wrong?" Fear throbbed in her chest. She'd never seen Terrence look like this. He appeared beaten down, defeated.

"Grandma Esther had another stroke and passed away last night. Her caretaker called me this morning." Saying the words brought fresh tears to his eyes.

"Oh no." Charisse brought her hands to her mouth.

As her eyes blurred with tears, Terrence stumbled into the house, clamped his arms around her waist, and buried his face in her neck. She fell against the wall and cupped the back of his head to offer comfort.

She shut her eyes, but the tears squeezed through—for the woman she came to love, and for the man holding onto her so tight. Grandma Esther had been mother and father to him and was his last closest relative.

She stroked his soft hair. "Oh, baby. I'm so sorry. I'm so, so sorry," she whispered.

⁂

HUNDREDS ATTENDED THE FUNERAL FOR ESTHER HYACINTH JONES, beloved by the people in her community, the church, and even those in the hip-hop community for her staunch support of her famous grandson.

The two-hour service included songs from the church choir and a word from her pastor about her years of service to the Lord by serving on committees to help the less fortunate. Only in recent years did she slow down, but continued to volunteer for hours every week by joining the outreach committee, where she made phone calls to follow up with members who were sick or hadn't been to service in a while.

Charisse sat in the front row, her children to the right, Terrence to her left. Chelsea clung to her and leaned on her arm. Terrence held fast to her hand.

During the eulogy, her heart broke when his voice thickened as he shared memories about the woman who took him in when he was twelve years old. Several times during the short speech, he glanced at Charisse and she smiled slightly, encouragingly, which seemed to give him strength. He would take a deep breath and follow through, his voice a little bit stronger.

The five of them stayed at the gravesite long after everyone else left. Chelsea sat in her father's lap with tear-streaked cheeks. The older boys lost their stoic expressions when their grandmother was lowered into the ground, so tears stained their cheeks, too.

They eventually left to join the attendees who were eating and drinking at the reception venue. But for the moment, the little family sat quietly and remembered Grandma Esther and her tart tongue, her wit, and her unconditional love for them all.

## ❧ 9 ❧

Terrence looked up when Charisse stepped out onto the back patio. He sat in the dark on one of the old wicker chairs Grandma Esther kept in the backyard, smoking a blunt to calm himself after spending the past four days in the company of concerned visitors he secretly wished would leave him alone so he could grieve in peace.

Charisse stayed behind to help him pack up his grandmother's belongings and mementos. Some of those items would be shipped back to his place in Atlanta, while others would be dumped or donated. Eventually, he'd have the place painted and cleaned in preparation for sale. There were minor repairs that needed to be done, too. The doorbell didn't work and there was a leak under the kitchen sink, but he was in no rush to get rid of the old brick house. There were too many memories and too much of his grandparents' history here.

Charisse walked behind him and sat down in the other wicker chair.

"How are the kids?" he asked. She'd called Atlanta to check on them.

"They're okay. Still sad about losing her, of course. Having a couple of days off from school was good for them, but they'll be going back tomorrow. Mom will make sure of that. Chelsea said to tell you that she loves you."

The corner of his mouth lifted up. "That's my princess," he said softly.

"What are we going to tackle next?" Charisse asked.

She was dressed down in a pair of thin, thigh-hugging sweats and a black T-shirt and wore her hair in two simple, large corn-rows. Yet he'd never wanted her more.

He appreciated her remaining behind to help, but her presence also inflicted torture. They hadn't stayed under the same roof in years. Even when they vacationed together, he rented separate lodging. So being in close proximity to her in the small house wore on his nerves. His gaze slid over her full breasts and he bit back a groan.

"The Salvation Army is coming to pick up the furniture tomor-row, but I need to pick up more boxes for the personal items. I guess I'll run and do that first thing in the morning, and then we can box up the rest of the stuff in the bedroom before starting on the attic. There's not much up there, so it shouldn't take long."

"Sounds good."

Terrence extended the blunt to her.

"I don't do this anymore," Charisse said, taking it.

"Give it back, then."

She eyed him. "Wait a minute. Let me get a few puffs."

"That's what I thought." He chuckled. "If my grandmother saw us right now, she'd be so pissed."

Charisse let smoke ease between her luscious lips. Damn, she was sexy. Spending the past four days with her in this house tested his control in unimaginable ways. She only had to stand in the same room with him, and every cell in his body went on high alert. Some days he wondered if he'd ever be able to feel, even remotely, for another woman the intense love and obsessive need he did for her. Maybe not—a just penance for all the dirt he'd done.

"I'll never forget that one time she caught us doing 'the reefer,'" she said.

Terrence laughed. "I forgot about that. Not in my house," he said, wagging a finger and mimicking Grandma Esther's voice.

"Then you had to go and say, 'But Grandma, we're outside.'" Charisse giggled and took another puff. "She almost knocked your head off with that pot."

"Who you telling? Hell, I can still hear her threatening me, talking 'bout, 'You ain't too grown for me to whoop your ass.'"

They both laughed then, and when they stopped, Terrence blinked back the tears that sprang to his eyes. Charisse handed him back the blunt and they sat in silence for a while.

"Thanks for staying with me," he said.

"Where else would I be, Terrence?"

"You could have left when the kids went back."

She shook her head. "I couldn't do that. I loved her too much. I want to make sure her house is packed up neatly."

"You saying I can't do that?" he asked teasingly.

"I'm saying you need my help."

She smiled at him, the way she used to, with affection in her eyes—before he blew up about her new man.

He rubbed away the pain in his chest. "Yeah, I do need you. Thanks, sweetheart."

۞

CHARISSE SLIPPED THE NIGHTSHIRT OVER HER HEAD AND THEN STEPPED over to the bathroom mirror. A refreshing shower had been what she needed after a long day packing and lugging boxes. Plus, she'd wanted to eliminate the pungent scent of weed smoke out of her skin.

There was only one bathroom in the little house, so while Terrence took a shower earlier, she put away the leftovers from dinner. He hadn't eaten much the past couple of days—at least not the way she knew he could eat. Hopefully, he'd regain his appetite soon.

She smoothed moisturizer into her face and tightened a silk

scarf over her braided hair. She picked up her discarded clothes and opened the door, and almost bumped into Terrence.

"Hey." He grabbed her arms.

She inhaled sharply and tensed but resisted the urge to withdraw from his touch. She became very conscious of her skimpy clothes. The thin nightshirt came to mid-thigh, and she wasn't wearing a bra. "Hey."

He was shirtless, and she clearly saw the tattoos on his chest and arms that were normally hidden under his clothes. Her gaze focused on the one on his left pec. *Charisse.*

After she confronted him about one of his women, he'd gotten it to prove her importance to him. She couldn't remember why she confronted him that time. Could have been because of a photo she saw online or rumors whispered throughout the music community.

*Right over my heart,* he'd said. A tribute to her. It was strange seeing the tattoo still there. She wondered why he never removed it or redesigned it into something else.

He dropped his hands. "Thought you were already in bed. I'm about to go to the kitchen and tear into that chicken you put away earlier."

"Got the munchies?" she teased.

"A little bit." He hesitated, as if he wanted to say something else. Then he shook his head. "Good night."

"Good night." She watched him walk away before going to the end of the hall. He'd given her his grandmother's bedroom, the largest in the house. She tossed the dirty clothes on top of the suitcase and climbed into bed. She didn't know how much sleep she'd get tonight. A restlessness filled her.

She must have dozed off at some point because she suddenly sensed she wasn't alone. Her eyes fluttered open in the dark, and she rolled onto her back. Terrence's dark figure hovered in the doorway.

"Terrence, what's wrong?"

"Mind if I come in and lay down with you for a minute? My mind won't let me rest."

She wanted to say no. The bed was small, only a full-size. But how could she refuse him in his time of need? "Of course not."

She turned on the bedside lamp and scooted over. He climbed onto the bed and lay on his back on the light comforter instead of sliding under the covers with her. He stared up at the ceiling, and she kept her gaze on him, noting his strong profile and the powerful display of his bare, muscled arms.

The restlessness came back, joined by the uncontrollable need to touch him. To caress his skin. He needed a friend right now, but lying in bed with him was doing strange things to her insides, despite the separation of the sheets between them.

"Doc said there was nothing they could do, but sometimes I wonder..." He frowned.

"Terrence," Charisse said, using the same voice she did when scolding their kids, "I hope you're not doing something foolish like blaming yourself. You did everything you could. You gave Grandma Esther the best care money could buy." She was never the same after the first stroke, and Charisse couldn't imagine there was anything else that could be done after the second.

He was silent for a moment. "Yeah," he finally said, his mouth twisting into a rueful smile. He turned onto his side so they faced each other. "You weren't around in the beginning, but she was so proud of me. When I won my first cypher contest, she invited over friends and the whole neighborhood for a cookout. She hooked it up! And she wouldn't let me pay for a thing, because she said it wouldn't be a gift if I had to contribute. She was the best publicist, too." He laughed softly to himself. "Used to talk me up to everybody, including the church folks."

"She did *not*. With all that cussing and sexual content in your songs?"

He chuckled. "She warned them but still let them know about my career, which she followed closer than I realized. Up until she passed, I can't believe she still cut articles about me out of the newspapers and magazines. Not the bad ones, though. She didn't like those."

"Oh, I remember. She really hated when they called you a thug. I think that upset her more than it did you."

"It did upset her. She used to chastise me in private about my behavior and warned me not to 'give them reporters nothing to write about.' She always had my back." Silence. "I wish she'd let me move her out of this old house."

"This is the house your grandfather bought for her. She was comfortable here, and think of all the memories of raising her daughter and raising you. I understand why she didn't want to move. At least she let you do some remodeling."

"But look how long that took. For years she told me to 'save your money, dear heart. Save it for your future.'"

"And you still do. So the constant nagging worked."

"I guess." He laughed a little. "Dang, I miss her."

"Me, too," Charisse whispered, tears filling her eyes. She kept her voice strong because she was supposed to be comforting him.

His gaze flicked over her, eyes softening. "Know what I wish I could have right now?"

"What?"

"One of your back rubs."

"That's not going to happen," Charisse said firmly. She was too fidgety and ill at ease and didn't quite know what to do with herself and the excess energy lying next to him evoked.

"Why not?"

"It's not a good idea, Terrence. You know that." She picked at a loose thread in the comforter.

"I know. But you give the best back rubs. Shit feels so good." His voice went lower. "I always feel good when I'm with you."

Charisse continued plucking at the thread, but his words sparked pain in her chest, and she bit down on her bottom lip to fight back tears. Allowing him into the room had definitely been a bad idea. She hated what he said, because those words filled her with regret and made her feel sorry for him, when she was the one who had been hurt, and she'd had every right to walk away from their marriage.

*What if he's changed?* a voice in her head whispered. But she couldn't risk the pain again.

Terrence took her hand loosely in his. "I'm not saying these things to upset you. I want you to know how special you are to me. I appreciate you staying behind to help me out. Grandma Esther always loved you. When she was in the hospital, she gave me hell about how I'd messed things up with you. She loved you like a daughter."

"I loved her, too."

Charisse withdrew her hand from his and curled it into a ball. Lying together in this bed, they were playing with fire. Cutting off contact was a necessity, or she might do something foolish. To change the subject to a safer topic, she said, "I loved her ginger-snap cookies, and the way the house smelled when she baked."

"Them dang cookies were the best. She didn't bake as much in recent years, but for my birthday last year, she baked me one of her apple pies."

Charisse stared at him. "Wait a minute, Grandma Esther baked you an apple pie and you didn't say anything?"

"Huh?" Faux-innocent eyes looked back at her.

"You heard me. Are you telling me you had one of her apple pies, and you didn't share?" His grandmother made the best apple pies she'd ever tasted, with the most amazing sugar-sprinkled crust.

"I thought you didn't want the kids to have too much sugar," Terrence said.

"Who's talking about the kids? I'm talking about me. You know how much I love her pies. Did you eat the whole thing by yourself?"

"*Hello...*"

"Oh my goodness!" Charisse shoved him and turned onto her other side, giving him her back.

"Hold up. It was *my* birthday," Terrence said.

"I don't care," Charisse said over her shoulder. "You know much I loved her baking, especially her apple pie. The fact that you ate the whole pie yourself and didn't save me a slice, shows exactly the kind of person you are. You are greedy. That's what it boils down to."

"Come on, don't be like that. Besides, I didn't eat the whole thing by myself. Grandma shared a slice with me." He flung an arm across her body and rested his chin on her arm. His touch heated her skin through the thin layer of clothes.

"Get off me, Terrence. Go back to your room."

"I'm hurting. My grandmother passed."

Charisse remained silent.

"You're not going to give me the silent treatment, are you?"

She didn't reply.

"You know I don't tolerate that," he warned.

Charisse shook him off, fluffed the pillow, and resettled on the bed. She closed her eyes.

"You know what's coming," Terrence warned.

Charisse's eyes flew open. "Don't you dare—"

His fingers dug into her sides, and a round of tickling began. Gasping, Charisse did her best to fight him off, but he was relentless.

"Say you forgive me," he said, sliding on top of her.

She refused at first but finally relented. "Okay, okay!" She could barely breathe for laughing so hard. "I forgive you."

He stopped, and they both simply looked at each other. The blanket continued to separate them, but one of his legs was lodged between her thighs. He rested on his elbows, but the weight from the lower part of his body bore down on her. That bout of tickling had made her core unexpectedly warm and wet. Why couldn't she make this ache go away? It constantly gnawed at her.

"I wasn't kidding with what I said earlier," Terrence said quietly.

"About what?" Charisse swallowed, a deep pain appearing

behind the walls of her abdomen. Something was happening between them. She feared it at the same time she welcomed it.

"I always feel better when I'm with you."

He lowered his head hesitantly at first. When she didn't move, he kissed her, and the world stood still for a split second before an explosion of sensation detonated in her body.

## ❧ 10 ❧

Charisse panted into his mouth. She wanted him desperately. She never wanted anyone the way she wanted this man, and despite her better judgment, she had to have him. *Now.*

It didn't take much to get her naked. Terrence worked her panties past her hips and slipped off the nightshirt with ease. He tossed the clothes to the side and then hurriedly removed his own and tossed them aside, too. When they were both stripped bare, he stared at her body in wonder.

"I never thought I'd see you like this again."

A frisson of desire sparked in her loins when he looked at her like that, but she didn't have time to think, much less respond. His lips pressed to hers, meshing their mouths in a searing kiss that stole her breath and made her dizzy with pleasure. The taste of him was incredible. Like something new and different, yet familiar. Her fingers skated over his soft, wavy hair, and all four limbs wrapped around him like tentacles while she kissed him deep, stroking the inside of his mouth with her tongue.

Terrence relinquished her lips and made his way to the middle of her breasts. He fastened on each one in turn, sucking each nipple while flicking the swollen tip with his tongue. They became his singular focus for a while. With gentle tugs from his teeth and kneading fingers, he treated them to exquisite torture. She arched into the merciless onslaught, rounding her back into a sharp curve to meet the demands of his mouth.

When he'd had his fill, Terrence cupped her sex with a possessive hand and kissed her stomach. Deft fingers spread her lower lips in preparation for what she knew was about to come.

His mouth moved lower, and he ran his nose along her inner thigh. He inhaled deeply. "You smell so good," he whispered huskily.

Terrence licked his lips as she closed her eyes, unable to bear looking as he bent his head toward her aching flesh. He cradled her bottom in his hands and when he placed a teasing lick to her sensitive sex, intense sensations exploded on her skin. He slid his tongue in. She let out a low moan and pressed her hand to the back of his head, fingers digging into his scalp as she silently pleaded for him to send her over the edge.

She spread her thighs without prompting and let him have his way with her. Each ragged gasp signaled her pleasure as his swirling tongue took her closer to heaven. He growled in appreciation as he plundered her slick flesh and owned her with his mouth. Tasting and licking. Nibbling and sucking.

"You taste so good. So sweet. I could never have enough of you."

She'd received oral sex from other men, but Terrence was so enthusiastic, turning an already sensual act into something so raw and carnal, he turned her on in a way other men didn't. She rotated her hips against his mouth, and when he squeezed her butt cheeks, the combined pressure of his hands at her back and his mouth at her front sent her careening over the edge of bliss.

She cried out and clawed the mattress. Mindlessly, she arched upward, panting so hard she was certain the harsh breaths scored her throat. When he finally released her, she settled back down.

She came so fast she was almost embarrassed, but it couldn't be helped. Terrence was good, and more than five years had passed since he made love to her. The accumulation of random touches, nighttime phone conversations, and laughter prompted by inside jokes banked up during all that time, waiting for this very moment.

Smoothing his hands over her thighs and pelvis, he came back up. "You still got that bomb pussy. Just delicious," he whispered. Then he pushed the scarf from her head and slid his fingers over her hair.

Grasping her head, he kissed her with tongue, swallowing her mouth with a greedy, wet kiss. He bit her chin and sucked on the side of her neck.

His hands once again moved to her breasts—massaging, kneading, squeezing.

"Terrence..."

"Tell me what you want."

"You." That had always been an issue when they made love. No matter how much he gave, she always wanted more.

She reached between his legs and closed her fingers around his impressive size. He closed his eyes and winced like someone in pain.

"You got me, Charisse." He opened his eyes and looked deeply into hers. "Always."

He nudged her legs apart and pushed into her. Every molecule, every cell, ceased movement in that moment.

Long and thick, he filled her to capacity. With an openmouthed groan, she let him know how good he felt.

"Damn, I miss fucking you." His words hit the side of her neck. He groaned as he continued to slide into her with deliciously long strokes.

Her fingers sank into his firm bottom and she rose to meet him.

"That's it. Give it to me," he encouraged roughly. He sucked air between his teeth.

"Terrence," she whimpered. His slow movements were driving her insane.

"I know, sweetheart. Feels good, don't it?" he whispered. He kissed her arched throat, and her fingers dug into his upper spine.

"Yes. You feel so good. You always feel so good."

Her hands wandered over his beautiful dark skin. She wanted to touch him everywhere.

She slid her hands over his obliques and across his back. His smooth skin was soft and warm to the touch. In continuous slow motion, he slid up into her aroused flesh. With his knees far apart, he kept her splayed wide for his pleasure while he took his time to savor the moment. He sank his teeth into her shoulder, and her nails raked his back as she met each thrust, desperate to control the speed but he refused to let her.

"You ready, sweetheart? You ready to come again?"

She whimpered an answer because she couldn't talk. She could only think about the connection they shared and the sweet friction between her legs.

He rotated a thumb over her hard right nipple and his hips lunged faster as he picked up the pace.

She found his mouth, using a hand at the back of his head to force him to kiss her. Their mouth-to-mouth contact was erotic, setting aflame her already heated body. Her other hand wrapped around his neck, holding him close as she kept time with each pump of his pelvis.

Terrence sank into her in a relentless pattern and she came hard, quivering around him. Her nails dug into her palm and a sharp cry split the air. She turned her nose to his throat and forced his head lower. She needed him closer, needed to meld their bodies into one being. She whispered his name like a prayer as a tidal wave of pleasure billowed through her body.

He groaned and came, too. The sound was guttural and harsh. There was nothing sexier than hearing him lose control like that. Clutching the pillow and arching his back, he emptied inside her.

He collapsed with a shudder. For a moment, only their heavy breathing could be heard.

"I love you so much."

Charisse pretended not to hear the words he whispered, but she kept her arms wrapped around him, holding on tight for a little bit longer.

## ❧ 11 ❧

Charisse stared up at the ceiling and listened to Terrence in the bathroom down the hall. She still felt him between her legs, his mouth on her skin, his hands kneading her breasts.

What had they done? They'd had sex, that's what they'd done. She'd loved every minute of it, but they needed to talk. He had a woman in his life, and she had a man in her life. They had messed up.

The years since the divorce helped dull the ache in her chest, and except for most recently, the smiles came easier and more naturally. She couldn't go back down the road of misery and pain she left behind years ago.

Terrence reentered the room and she held her breath, mind racing to find the right words. She closed her eyes to buy herself more time, but when he climbed onto the bed, he pulled off the covers, and her eyes flew open.

Before she could protest, he used a warm wet washcloth to clean her up, sending a renewed surge of heat through her still sensitive flesh. He tended to her with such care, she simply lay there, watching him. When he finished, he set the washcloth aside.

"Better?" he asked.

"Mhmm."

They lay on their sides, both uncovered, both naked. Her nipples were hard and her body hummed from the pleasurable lovemaking, but she remained still. She hated him a little bit. Why did he have to be such a good lover? Why couldn't any other man make her go through the same intense, almost violent waves of passion he awakened inside her?

"You're so gorgeous, you know that?" Terrence whispered.

"Thank you."

Her fingertip traced her name written in cursive on his skin. Didn't his lovers have a problem with him having his ex-wife's name tattooed on his chest?

"I can't believe you never covered this."

"Told you I'd never cover it. You didn't believe me?"

"I guess I'm surprised."

Whenever he posed shirtless for the gram—hanging with the fellas, during a workout on the set of a video shoot, or partying at some other celebrity's pad—her name was obvious for the general public to see. Right after the divorce, occasionally interviewers asked if he would cover it up.

"Why would I?" he'd retort, and he'd mean-mug them, daring them to pursue that line of questioning. The stare off usually ended with the reporter laughing uncomfortably and saying something like, "Just asking." Then they'd move on to the next topic.

After a few of those awkward moments, he was never asked about her name on his chest again.

"We need to talk," Charisse said.

"About what?"

"About what happened tonight."

"What happened is that we had sex."

"I *know*." She took a deep breath and closed her eyes, then reopened them. "But what we did—"

"Shh." He scooted down in the bed and pressed his lips to her hip. His moist tongue lapped the curve of her skin, and she closed her eyes, shuddering and wanting more.

"Terrence, we can't. We can't do this."

"We already did. What's one more time?"

Her throbbing core agreed with him.

He came higher and covered her right breast with his hand. He knew that was the most sensitive one, so he'd basically declared war on her resistance.

He kissed her neck, and she arched into his lips and the squeeze of his hand. She let him suck his way down to her breasts. He squeezed them both together and when he fanned his tongue across the swollen tip of the right one, she almost came. Gasping, she clutched the back of his head.

She wanted him. Oh god, how she wanted him again. Over and over. As much as he would give her. The greedy little monster between her legs hadn't had nearly enough.

"Terrence, wait..."

"Hmm?" His teeth grated over the tip of her breast, and she shivered.

*Focus.* She pushed at his shoulders and he reluctantly released the nipple, a lazy smile crossing his lips.

Finally able to breathe easier, Charisse met his gaze. "We have to talk about this."

"What is there to talk about?"

"You're hurting right now. You're not thinking straight."

"I'm thinking straight. I told you before we came here that I wanted another chance with you."

"Okay fine, I'm not thinking straight!" She needed to get through to him.

He smirked. "We had a good sex life, and tonight proves we still have that fire. Why you want to fight this when it feels so good?" He slid a hand between her legs and fingered her moist flesh. "Give me one good reason why I should stop kissing on you, loving on you, when we both want it."

She stilled his hand. "I'm with someone else, Terrence. You know that."

His features hardened in an instant and he rolled off her onto his back. He stared up at the ceiling.

"I'm sorry," she whispered.

"You think I want to talk about your man while I'm lying in bed with you? I bet you weren't thinking about him a minute ago when you were tearing up my back."

True, and that made her feel guilty. "So you think good sex is all that matters?"

"It's not all that matters, but..." He rose up on an elbow and let his gaze sweep down her body. She moved to cover her breasts and he smacked her hand away. "Since when do you hide from me? You belong to him now, is that it?"

"I never said—"

He rolled onto her and pinned her arms on either side of her head. "You worried about that Austin nigga? You think I care?" He kneed her thighs apart and his erection pressed against her abdomen like a hot rod.

"Terrence—"

"I know what you like," he said, head bent to her ear. "I know when you want it hard or soft. I know when you want gentle or rough. I know every mole on your body and every stretch mark you gained carrying my babies. And I know you want more of this dick."

His warm breath brushed the sensitive lobe of her ear. She closed her eyes tight, willing her body to resist, but knowing she wouldn't. It had been too long since she experienced this type of passion. It had been too long since she'd been with the only man who could turn her inside out with a simple look.

He was right. He knew her like no one else, and that made him irresistible.

"I don't give a fuck about your man," he said.

His hands were rougher this time. But rough or gentle, Terrence gave unsurpassed pleasure, every touch inflicting a riot of sensation that turned her into a wanton, moaning fraction of herself, willing to surrender all to him.

He flipped her onto her stomach and pushed her legs apart.

Then his weight came down on top of her as he slid between her thighs. Charisse gripped the bedsheets, whimpering and trembling as his steely length filled her.

His body plowed into hers, his fingers sank into her hair. They fastened around a braid and he pulled back her head. "You're mine tonight," he growled.

Over and over his hardness plunged into the depths of her body. The small bed rocked with each deep, pounding stroke. There was anger in each thrust. Anger and a need to possess.

Charisse met his need with a need of her own. Her hips bounced up to meet his solid drives. Reaching back, she grabbed his ass and then clenched her muscles around his hard shaft.

The rhythm of his hips faltered and he muttered an expletive. "Charisse," he groaned.

Yes, she belonged to him tonight. But he belonged to her, too.

He pressed his face into the side of her neck and slid a hand down to her clit. He started moving again. All the while he played with the little damp bundle of nerves. He needed to push her faster toward climax so he wouldn't come before she did.

Mere seconds later, the wave of an orgasm undulated from where Terrence was buried inside her, and rippled with great force throughout her entire body. She cried out in relief. Overwhelmed. Overjoyed. Completely consumed.

He continued to ride her as wave after wave seized her muscles. "That's it, sweetheart," he said in a hoarse, trembling voice.

Then he came, too, with a loud shout. His arms crushed her to him as he rammed into her over and over.

Their ravenous appetite for each other ended with them both collapsed on the bed, panting, spent, and sated.

CHARISSE REMAINED UNMOVING IN BED, LISTENING TO THE STILLNESS of late morning. She knew it was late because sunlight poured through the sheer drapes. She and Terrence spent most of the night screwing like they only had twenty-four hours to live and the survival of humanity depended on them.

Her bottom and legs butted up against his warm body, and she knew without turning over that he was awake.

"Morning," he said, his voice a rough rasp. He knew she was awake, too.

"Morning," she replied.

Terrence moaned and the bed moved as he stretched. Then a heavy dark arm landed across her waist and he nuzzled her shoulder blade.

"Feel so good waking up next to you," he whispered.

Her hand covered his. Though conflicted about what to do next, she enjoyed this moment, too. Waking up next to him was comforting and didn't feel odd or peculiar.

She knew he'd dozed off when his even breathing sounded in the room. What seemed like only minutes later, her eyes flew open. She'd fallen asleep, too, at some point, exhausted from the night of sexual gymnastics. But a noise woke her up. She cocked her head.

Someone was in the house.

"Terrence," she whispered in a panic, nudging him with an elbow.

"What's—"

"Shh!" Charisse whispered fiercely. "There's someone in the house."

"T?" a female voice said a distance away. She recognized that voice. It was Kim, his current flame. What was she doing here?

"Oh, shit," Terrence muttered. He sat up in the bed, obviously intending to stop her in the hall, before she came into the room.

"Babe, you here?" Kim called. She pushed on the slightly ajar door.

Charisse's eyes widened and she scrunched down into the sheets, wishing she could disappear.

Kim halted before she stepped a foot over the threshold, mouth falling open. "What's going...?" She stared at them in bed together.

"You son of a bitch!" she screamed. "I thought I would surprise you." Tears filled her eyes. She looked at him, then Charisse, then him again. "You didn't want me to come because you knew you'd be here with *her*. You're despicable!"

"Kim, listen to me—" Terrence said.

"I hate you!" she screamed.

She swung around and rushed down the hall.

Charisse covered her head with the blanket and closed her eyes. If Kim had snatched the linens from the bed and scratched her eyes out, she wouldn't have blamed the younger woman.

"Hold on!" she heard Terrence call. "Charisse, I'll be right back."

He scrambled from the bed. Movement in the room suggested he'd gathered his pants and put them on. The bedroom door slammed, and seconds later muffled yelling came from the front of the house as Kim and Terrence argued outside.

Charisse wanted to die. She'd done something so vile, she didn't know if she could look at herself later.

She'd become the other woman.

## ❧ 12 ❧

"Well, your life might be in shambles, but you look great." Vicky, Charisse's friend and hairstylist, stood back and assessed her handiwork.

"Thanks," Charisse said dryly.

Vicky smiled then twisted her around in the chair so she could face the mirror.

Charisse fluffed the shiny strands and shook her head from side to side so her hair bounced. She had been overdue for a visit to the salon, and her friend did a great job as usual. She'd given Charisse a retouch, applied a semi-permanent color to enrich her natural hue, and sewn in a couple of blonde tracks to layer in brightness to her hair.

The effect was amazing. She looked younger and refreshed. Very important, since her face was once again showing up regularly online.

Ever since the fiasco in Macon, Kim had been making the rounds, telling anyone who'd listen that her boyfriend, T-Murder, broke her heart. Terrence claimed to Charisse that he and Kim were not in a relationship and merely hooked up every now and again. Kim clearly saw their "hookups" differently and posted a video with tears in her eyes, bemoaning the fact that she found the man she thought she had a future with in bed with his ex-wife. She was particularly devastated since she went to Macon to console him after the death of his grandmother.

The doorbell hadn't worked, and she tried the door and unfortunately for Charisse and Terrence, found it unlocked. No doubt because they'd both paid little attention to locking up when they'd been buzzing off "the reefer." So that's how Kim managed to enter the house and discover them in bed together.

Charisse knew better than to follow the story, but she nonetheless checked the usual places online. When she saw the photos of herself, a couple obviously taken through long-range camera lenses, she'd been annoyed and appalled at her appearance. For the next few weeks at least, while this woman made her rounds and Charisse had somehow become public enemy number one, she wanted to look her best while being disparaged online.

Vicky brushed fine hairs off her shoulders. "How do you feel now?"

"Like a new woman."

"Well, you look great."

"Thanks to you." Minutes later, she handed Vicky a hefty tip. "See you in a couple of months."

"Take care of yourself, girl." Her friend's eyes filled with sympathy.

"I'll try."

Charisse went to the front, avoiding eye contact with the other patrons on the way, and paid for her services. Her security detail, a large white man who stood out like an orange in a bushel of apples, left the chair he sat in while Vicky did her hair, and came to stand near her. She donned large sunglasses and walked a block to the black SUV parked at the curb. The bodyguard opened the back door and she slipped in, safely ensconced behind tinted windows. Then he climbed in the front with the driver.

She returned to Atlanta the same day Kim discovered her and Terrence but hadn't seen him since they parted over a week ago. They'd spoken on the phone twice since then. On the last call he insisted that not only would the kids have security, but he didn't want Charisse driving and would assign her a bodyguard for when she left the house, until the hoopla surrounding the scandal died down.

She'd spent years out of the spotlight and grew accustomed to driving wherever she needed to go, but because she'd unexpectedly been thrust back into the public eye with such force, she agreed with Terrence. Her nerves were a mess, and she worried each time she stepped foot in public, someone would secretly take a photo of her and post it online, or she'd be approached by curious fans or an aggressive reporter. Knowing the kids were safe and having someone else responsible for taking her back and forth and escorting her to her destinations around the city made life a little easier and gave her one less thing to worry about.

She walked into the house at twelve-thirty, fixed a simple omelette and fruit lunch, and then sat down at the counter to eat. The kids were all going over to friends' houses after school and wouldn't be home until dinner, so she had plenty of time to catch up on bills and send a couple of emails.

At one thirty, the intercom buzzed and she checked the monitor. Terrence stood outside at the door. What was he doing here?

He looked up at the camera, and her heart tightened. Memories of the night they spent together came rushing back, and her skin heated as if he was standing right there, caressing her body all over again.

She could feel him inside of her. Could taste the saltiness of his skin and experience the almost violent way he shoved into her as he growled his need into her ear, alternating between devastatingly slow strokes and mind-blowingly heavy thrusts.

Charisse fanned her face and breathed slowly from her mouth to calm down. At this rate, she'd spontaneously combust before he stepped foot in the house.

She pressed the intercom button. "Use your key," she said.

She worried about her reaction to seeing him in the flesh again, but they needed to talk about the explosion in the media and their supposedly rekindled relationship.

Terrence entered the house and came back to the kitchen. His wavy hair looked freshly trimmed, lined up around the edges and a little higher on top.

"Hey."

"Hey," she replied. She stood.

"You got your hair done. Looks nice." His gaze trailed over her skinny jeans, and whatever he was thinking made him bite his bottom lip before their eyes met again.

Her cheeks heated. "Thank you. Your trim looks nice, too."

"How you been?" he asked. He looked so good in loose-fitting jeans and a white V-necked tee that hugged his body and created a sharp contrast against his dark umber skin.

Charisse smoothed clammy hands over her hips. "How do you think I've been? You know I hate having my name mentioned on TMZ or shared anywhere online, but what can we do? Your girlfriend has turned our private life into an opportunity for publicity and online clout."

He ran a wary hand over the back of his head. His tattoo-covered biceps flexed. "I told you before she's not my girlfriend, and don't worry—she'll go away soon. Her fifteen minutes of fame will soon be up."

She eyed him, dissatisfied with that answer. She wished they could make Kim and all the salacious gossip go away overnight.

"What do you want me to say, Charisse? We worked toward this type of fame at one time, remember? We can't turn it on and off anytime we want. We both knew publicity was part of the deal. What's going on in our lives will always be interesting to the general public."

"I'm not part of that life anymore. I don't want to be a part of it. I don't want to be a part of the media circus that's *your* life. That's why I live out here, but you're dragging me back into it."

"So you regret what happened between us?" He tilted his head, his voice low and warm.

"Of course I do."

"I thought once you had time to think, you'd see things differently."

"I don't."

"We made love, like we used to, and it was good. You enjoyed it, and I enjoyed it." His eyes darkened. "I want to put my mouth on you and feel you under me again. It's so damn hard not to reach for you right now."

She knew that feeling, because she wanted to reach for him, too. "Stop talking to me like that."

His eyes focused on her breasts, and she wondered if he could see how hard her nipples were through her blouse. She was too afraid to look and hoped the hunger she experienced the minute she saw his face on the monitor hadn't manifested in that way.

"How are things with Dud—I mean, Austin?"

"Over." After a particularly awkward conversation, Austin walked away and left Charisse to wallow in the aftertaste of guilt as a result of betraying someone who'd been nothing but good to her.

"Can't say that I'm sorry." His expression was totally unrepentant.

Charisse took a deep breath and placed her hands on her hips. "Why did you come here?"

"I was worried about you."

"You could have inquired about my well-being over the phone. As you can see, I'm fine."

"Yes, you are." His gaze trailed over her again, and this time his nostrils flared.

He'd used one of the oldest lines in the book, and still she blushed, as if he'd recited original poetry.

Terrence came closer, and her core spasmed in a silent cry for him. He stopped within arm's length of her. "I'm not fine, though. I miss you. I need you. Right this minute."

She reached back and gripped the counter. Would one more time really hurt?

He eased closer, deep into her personal space. He brushed his lips to her cheek. With his mouth hovering over hers, he whispered, "You know you own me. Heart, body, and soul."

She lowered her gaze. The feeling was mutual. He owned her, inside and out, but she dared not admit it. She couldn't give him that kind of power again. His hands moved slowly to the front of her jeans, giving her ample time to stop him.

She didn't.

He unsnapped the button and lowered the zipper.

She let him.

He slipped a hand inside her panties and stroked a long finger at the cleft between her legs. He swore softly. "You been standing here being cold to me, but you're wet like this?"

When he pushed two fingers inside her, an involuntary gasp left her throat. She gripped his shoulders. He pushed the jeans lower and grabbed her bottom and squeezed. He hauled her against his body, and her arms slid around his neck.

Terrence licked her lower lip and then slid his tongue across the edge of her teeth. She moaned, rising up on tiptoe and seizing the pink snake between her lips. One hand caressed his wide neck and slipped up into his freshly cut hair.

"One time, Terrence. That's it," she whispered against his mouth.

He laughed softly, sexy and confident as he looked down at her from narrowed eyes dark with lust. He kissed below her jaw and shoved a hand into her hair. "I already know the kids won't be home for hours. And you know good and well this ain't no one-time afternoon."

He covered her mouth, kissing her deep and hard. Her passionate response matched his. She rubbed her hips against him and let her hands smooth under his shirt and caress his warm, firm skin. She pressed closer, opening her mouth and tilting back her head to deepen the kiss.

He was right. Once wouldn't be enough.

Not for a long time to come.

## ❧ 13 ❧

There was something about laying naked across the bed with your head on your man's abs while he smoothed a firm hand from the base of your neck to the middle of your shoulder blades in a soothing, repeated motion. For the past five weeks, Terrence made the trip north of the city two nights a week to slip into the house undetected so they could make love.

Tonight made the third night for the week because tomorrow he left for Louisiana to film his part in another action film coming out next year. It was his biggest role to date, and not only was he excited, Charisse was excited too. This role could open up additional doors for him to enter into acting once he left music. The new challenge stoked his creative juices, and he now took acting lessons to hone his craft.

"You should come with me," Terrence said.

"I would love to, but I have so much to do."

"You don't have to come out for the entire two weeks I'll be there. Come out for a few days and stay at the Hilton with me. While I'm on set, you could go on sightseeing tours. You like history, so you could check out the Whitney Plantation. Isn't that the one you said you wanted to visit one day? At night we could go out and try new restaurants, maybe do some dancing..."

All of that sounded enticing, but she had too much to do with the kids and the landscaping project she still needed to make a decision about. "I'll have to see. Maybe I can come for a couple of days."

He stroked the depths of his fingers through her messy hair, brushing the strands back from her face. "I'd like that."

Before she could respond, the doorknob rattled. "Mommy, the door is locked." The doorknob rattled again. "Mommy." Her daughter's pleading voice came through from outside in the hall.

Charisse's head popped up and she looked at Terrence.

He let his head fall back against the headboard. "You gotta put a stop to this," he said wearily.

"I know. But I have to let her in, which means you have to go."

He stared at her. "I'm not leaving."

"Mommy, the door is locked. I can't get in." Chelsea's voice came louder.

"Yes, you are," Charisse whispered. "We agreed we wouldn't let the kids see you here at night. Coming, princess. Give me a minute."

She scurried off the bed and picked up her silk robe from the trunk. "Chop, chop, hurry up. Go out the French doors and walk around the back to the front of the house."

"This is ridiculous," Terrence grumbled.

He got down off the bed, completely naked. She paused, ogling his toned back and admiring the way his dark skin glowed under the limited light in the room. His body, though not as tight as his younger days when he worked out all the time, still contained visible muscles that moved under his skin, and he had a beautiful behind that she gripped with talon-like force multiple times tonight when he'd given her toe-curling orgasms.

"Where are my shoes?" Terrence asked, slipping a foot into his jeans.

"I don't know."

Chelsea banged on the door. "Mommy!"

"I'm coming!" She turned to Terrence. "Go, and I'll send them to you later."

"I'm not leaving this property without my shoes."

"Fine! I'll find them once I settle her down, but that might take a while."

"I'll wait on the back deck, and you can bring them to me."

"Okay. Go." She pushed him out the French doors and locked up. The motion lights came on, and his figure moved across the grass in the direction of the kitchen.

Charisse hurried toward the bedroom door and tripped over one of Terrence's shoes. "Wonderful. There's one of them," she muttered.

She opened the door and Chelsea scowled at her. "The door was locked. I couldn't get in," she said in an accusatory tone. She swept in like the princess she believed herself to be.

Charisse sighed. They were creating a monster.

Chelsea climbed into the bed and under the covers. "Was Daddy here?"

Charisse stopped in her tracks. "What?"

Chelsea sniffed the pillowcase. "The pillow smells like Daddy."

"Go to sleep," Charisse said.

She climbed into bed with her daughter, and Chelsea snuggled up next to her and flung an arm over her throat. Within a few minutes, she was fast asleep.

Charisse waited a few more minutes to make sure that she was in deep slumber before she slipped out from under her arm. Tiptoeing around the room, she located Terrence's discarded shoes and then quietly left the room and closed the door.

In the kitchen, she opened the back door and let him in, handing over the shoes. "It's safe to come in now. She's asleep."

"Thank you," he said dryly. He closed the door and locked it. "You know you need to put a stop to her, right?"

"Yes, I know, but it's hard."

"How hard can it be? You tell her she has to sleep in her own room. She never did this when you and I were married. She knows she can get away with it because you let her. See where all this princess talk got you?" He bent over to put on his shoes.

"Me?" Charisse said in an incredulous whisper. "You're the one who bought her three tiaras. That's what started the downward spiral into princess entitlement."

"If I started it, I'll put an end to it. I'll have a talk with her." Terrence straightened, now fully dressed. "I better go. You got any bottled water?"

"Chilled or room temperature?"

"Chilled."

"I should have a few in the fridge." Charisse shuffled over and checked. "Flavored or unflavored?"

"Unflavored. What's this?"

She removed one of the bottles and faced him. He picked up the proposal for the landscaping design that the yard guy brought over. "Something Tony put together for me. I want to spruce up the yard."

"Have you gotten any other estimates?" Terrence flipped through the pages.

"No. I let Tony handle everything. You know how I am. I don't like to deal with that kind of thing, and he was really nice and helpful with the whole process."

She tried her hand at being an entrepreneur several times, and Terrence invested in every one of her failed businesses during their marriage—a hair salon, a children's boutique, a coffee shop, and a lingerie store. All failed miserably because she simply didn't have the managerial skills or the business acumen to make them work.

"I bet he was." He didn't sound convinced. "I don't understand why I haven't seen this before. It's dated three weeks ago. You know what, never mind. I'll have Kamisha do some checking and make sure Tony hasn't inserted a commission into these quotes for his *help*." He took a gulp of water. "I still don't understand why you didn't tell me about your plan to do work on the yard."

"Because I'm paying for it."

He frowned. "With what money? You don't work."

"I'm going to use some of the money you give me every month."

"That's *your* money."

"I *know*."

"So if you know, what are you talking about? That money is for you to do whatever you want with. We have an agreement. I take care of the house and the bills and what you need for the kids."

"I know. But..." She looked away.

Terrence tilted up her chin. "But when you decided to do this, we were angry at each other, and you thought you couldn't come to me."

"It didn't feel right, Terrence."

"I don't care how it *feels*. I told you I'd always take care of you, and I meant it. I want to. I want to because I love you, and I don't want you to need anything at all. That doesn't change because we're fighting. Whatever you need, I got you."

"You can't take care of me forever."

"Says who?"

She let out a pained sigh. "One day you'll get married and your new wife is not going to be okay with you supporting me."

"I'll continue doing whatever I please, and this hypothetical woman will just have to deal."

He tucked the proposal under his arm. "I'll take care of this."

"What if I remarry?"

He halted on the way out. Silence filled the kitchen. Charisse stared at his broad back, waiting for him to turn around, but he didn't.

Finally, he said, "We'll cross that bridge when we get to it."

He continued to the front of the house, and she followed. There was so much more she wanted to say but didn't know how.

"Terrence," she whispered.

He turned around and looked at her for a moment with sadness in his eyes. "I know."

Her heart broke a little.

He closed the gap between them in the dark hallway and clasped the side of her neck. "I know we're not back together, and I know I still have a lot of work to do. I don't take you for granted, and I'll keep putting in the work to prove that I've changed, and you can trust me again. But...even if you don't give us another chance, I want you to know that I love you, and when I say I'll take care of you, I mean it. So let me have that, okay? It's the one thing I ever did right with us, so... Let me do this."

His eyes begged her to give in, and she nodded. "Okay," she said softly.

"Which design do you like best?" he asked just as softly.

"It doesn't matter—"

"Which design do you like best?"

"The third one." It was the most expensive but included everything she wanted.

"Then that's the one you'll have."

He gently kissed her lips and held his mouth pressed to hers for a long moment. Then he rested his forehead against hers. "I love you. No matter what happens between us, even if you never take me back, I love you. That will never change."

He stepped away and left quietly out the door.

Charisse didn't go back to bed. She walked into the kitchen and watched him on the monitor, ambling down the driveway with his delicious walk, like he owned the universe. He rounded the bend and disappeared from sight, where he'd parked so the kids wouldn't know he was there.

Hands braced on the counter, Charisse bowed her head under the grip of strong emotion. Was she being too hard on him? She finally admitted to herself that she still loved him, too. She wanted so badly to tell him. She physically ached to say the words but worried about what such an admission would mean.

Capitulation. Giving in to emotion instead of listening to reason. Letting her heart control her behavior—a bruised and battered heart that seemed to be a glutton for punishment—

instead of using her brain to direct her actions. If only she had a sign to tell her what to do.

Go right or go left? Take him back or not? Play it safe or take the risk? She didn't know what to do.

"Send me a sign," she whispered.

## ❧ 14 ❦

"I can't hang with y'all, man. I'm old. I'm going back to the hotel."

Terrence had spent the past few hours eating and drinking with the crew and some of the other actors at a local restaurant. After dinner, they split into two groups. One group left to hit Bourbon Street, while he and seven others migrated over to the bar and stood around in a circle chatting some more.

But it was getting late, they had an early day tomorrow, and he wanted to practice his lines before going to bed.

"That, I don't believe. I know you party harder than this," said one of the actors.

Terrence chuckled and clapped him on the shoulder. "I know you know better than to believe everything you read in the tabloids, considering some of the stuff I've read about you."

Everyone in the small group chuckled.

"I'ma see y'all later. I'm out." He waved goodbye to them.

An actress with mocha-toned skin followed and placed a restraining hand on his arm. She stood on tiptoe. "Want some company, T-Murder?" she whispered, giving her bottom lip a seductive bite. She had a banging body and for the past week had made it clear she wanted to sleep with him.

"Nah, I'm good."

"You sure?" She arched a brow.

"Positive." He carefully removed her hand from his arm.

"If you change your mind, you know which room I'm in." He did know, because she'd told him.

Terrence nodded and then continued to walk out of the restaurant. He had no interest in taking her up on the offer.

He tugged his cap low on his brow so he couldn't be easily recognized and stepped out into the night with a little extra pep in his step. Charisse called earlier today and agreed to come see him late tomorrow. On his last two days on set, he'd have her with him, and he couldn't wait to hold her—something he hadn't been able to do for twelve long days. They agreed to stay a couple extra days to do some sightseeing and enjoy the nightlife.

Outside, the streets were packed, but he turned right and headed to his hotel. Soon he was walking through the doors of the Hilton.

Bo came rushing toward him. "Where you been? I called and sent a text. I been trying to reach you for the last hour."

"I had drinks with the crew after dinner." He pulled out his phone and saw the missed texts and calls. He never heard the phone over the din in the restaurant and bar. He tucked it into his back pocket. "What's the matter?"

"Gossip Bomb says they're printing an interview of your latest girlfriend, an Instagram model named JoJo. She said y'all are having an affair and you've put her up at hotels and flown her out to meet you."

"Who?" His mind was genuinely blank, but this could not be good.

"JoJo. I don't recognize her." Bo held up his phone and showed Terrence a picture he probably texted him earlier. She was a pretty young woman with pouty lips posing on a bed in lingerie for the camera. "They're going to print the interview without your comment if they don't hear from you, but they want a comment. You now have thirty minutes to respond."

Terrence cursed. He recognized her. "She's a liar. I'm not seeing anybody but my wife, and I barely knew this chick. We may have hooked up once, last year or something. Here in New Orleans, actually. Wait, now it's coming back to me. She was here for a concert, and I ran into her at one of the clubs. You weren't with me that time. She hung out with us in VIP and then... I took her back to the hotel. But I never saw her again after that. I sure as hell never flew her nowhere."

"Is that what you want me to tell Gossip Bomb?"

"Nah, you can tell them to go fuck themselves."

Bo sighed. "Whatever you say, Charisse is gonna see."

His stomach knotted up. He needed to think about her and how this could affect their already fragile relationship. He ran a hand down the back of his head. "Okay, I need to be careful. Call Hudson Lynch, tell him to prepare a statement for me." Hudson was his official spokesperson. "How much time do we have?"

Bo looked at his phone. "Twenty-five minutes."

"Let's hurry up and do this."

They rode the elevator to Terrence's floor. While Bo called Hudson, Terrence kneaded his temple where a headache emerged.

This couldn't be happening now, right when he saw the possibility of winning back his ex-wife. He'd have to do serious damage control. After he finished with Hudson, he'd call Charisse to warn her about the completely false story that was about to hit online.

The media storm with Kim would be nothing compared to the crap about to hit the fan if Charisse believed, even remotely, that he'd been secretly spending time with another woman while trying to woo her back into a relationship with him.

No matter what happened tonight, he hoped she believed him.

"Good afternoon, Mrs. Burrell."

Charisse smiled tightly at the activities coordinator as she strolled through her mother's building at the assisted living community. Even in a big floppy hat and shades, the woman recognized her. Maybe this "disguise" was a waste of time anyway. Did the seniors really care about what was going on in the life of a rapper and his ex-wife?

She took the elevator to the second floor and knocked before entering.

"I'm out here," her mother called outside the sliding glass door.

Charisse discarded the hat and glasses on the sofa and joined her mother on the balcony. Martha's concerned eyes followed her as she sat down at the little round table that looked out into the back courtyard.

"Thirsty?" Her mother waved at the two glasses.

"Thanks." Charisse drank half the glass of iced water and replaced it on the table.

"You're going to have to talk to him eventually," her mother said.

"I know. I'll talk to him when he gets back."

Ever since the news broke about Terrence's latest girlfriend, he'd been blowing up her phone. In the Gossip Bomb article, his spokesperson claimed he had not been involved with her since last year. However, JoJo provided a video of her and him going into a hotel together in New Orleans.

Charisse couldn't believe he asked her to come see him while he entertained another woman there. One scandal ended and another reared its ugly head. Of course, her name came up because only two months ago, the rumor was that they had reconciled. She was back in the news cycle again, and she was sick and tired of being sick and tired.

Terrence called five times and sent her numerous texts, the last one stating he was leaving early and on his way back so they could talk. She texted him back, insisting he meet his obligations on set and they could talk when he came into town on Sunday.

"I was looking forward to going to see him in New Orleans, spend time with him. Then this happened." She laughed shortly and shook her head.

Martha covered her hand. "I warned you. He hurt you before. He didn't respect your marriage."

"I know. You were right. I guess I wanted to believe that he changed."

"A leopard can't change his spots, baby. So you had sex with your ex-husband. If that's the worst of it, you'll be fine."

"That's not the worst of it," Charisse said quietly.

"What else is there?"

She looked at her mother. "I'm pregnant." She found out Thursday, which was why she'd wanted to fly to New Orleans to see Terrence. She couldn't wait to tell him the news and wanted to do it in person.

Martha's mouth fell open. "How?" She shook her head. "Never mind, I know how. But…weren't you careful?"

"No. I just didn't think."

"Obviously."

Her shoulders slumped. "Thanks, Mom."

"Well…" Her mother shrugged. "Maybe you wanted to get pregnant."

"*No.* I did not want to get pregnant."

"Then explain to me why you didn't use some kind of birth control. What did you think would happen? Did you forget how you ended up with the other three?"

"I don't know!" Charisse flung up her hands in exasperation. "I was foolish. Careless." She felt she was too old to be pregnant by accident, yet that's the predicament she found herself in.

"Okay, okay." Martha patted her hand.

"We were in a good place before."

"Real good, apparently."

"I mean before we slept together. I enjoyed the vacations we took, almost like we were a family again. I was excited about this year's trip. This year he planned to take us to the Galapagos Islands. Four days in Ecuador and ten days on the islands." She sighed. "Seeing him all the time and being friendly was hard, but doable. Sleeping with him was a mistake, and now this baby complicates everything."

"I do want another grandchild, but..." Martha sighed. "What are you going to do?"

"I want this baby."

"How do you think Terrence will feel?"

"He'll want it. I'm not worried about that. But he'll think a baby means we're getting back together and..."

"And you wanted that, too."

"I did." She blinked rapidly and bit into her bottom lip.

He penetrated the shield she put up to protect against him, and she'd fallen for him all over again. But in true Terrence form, he reminded her why they never worked the first time.

She'd always loved the bad boys when she was younger, especially those New York men. Their accent and swagger always did her in. Ennis's biological father had been from Queens, but he died unexpectedly from a ruptured spleen. Then she met Terrence, and he wowed her with that smile and made her believe they'd belong to each other until the end of time.

Even when she learned that wasn't true, she hung in there because he'd been good to her otherwise and loved her son as his own. Looking back, she couldn't believe she put up with his behavior for so long. She made her peace with the situation, convincing herself it was enough that he came home to her. It was enough that he wrote songs about her, shouted her out as his rock, his queen, his soulmate in almost every interview, and certainly every awards acceptance speech.

But those grand gestures weren't enough. They were never enough. She loved him, but he was bad for her. Bad for her heart and bad for her sanity.

"When am I going to learn? How old do I have to be before I finally get it? He's no good for me," she whispered, voice trembling.

Her mother caught her hand again and squeezed. "You get it

this time. Be strong and walk away from him on your terms, with your head up. Like you did before."

She nodded her agreement. That's all she could do.

Baby or not, she and Terrence were over.

She'd received her sign.

## ❧ 15 ❧

"**E**verything in that article is a lie."

Charisse had barely crossed the pristine hardwood floor of Terrence's swanky condo in West Buckhead when he blurted the words.

She dropped her purse onto the circular bar that separated a large kitchen filled with Bosch appliances from the living room filled with white furniture and windows that spanned from the ceiling to the floor as they looked out onto the city. At least he hadn't tried to touch her, for which she was glad.

"I'm fine and how are you?" she asked in a pleasant voice.

Terrence studied her for a moment. He didn't look so good, and she secretly reveled in his distress. Why should she be the only one upset? She hoped he hadn't slept a wink in the hours leading up to this meeting, as he wondered whether or not he'd be able to lie his way out of this particular mess.

"I'm fine," he said.

"How did things go on the set?"

"That's not why you came here."

"I'm *trying* to have a normal conversation. Do you not want to tell me how filming went?"

He scrubbed a hand down his face. "All right...filming went

well. I think I'm really getting the hang of this acting thing. Crew was great, everything was great." He swallowed. "Do you want to sit down?"

"No. This won't take long."

"Charisse..."

"I don't want to talk about your latest girlfriend."

"We have to talk about it, and she's not my latest girlfriend. You're the only woman in my life. JoJo lied. That video is not from last week or the week before. It has to be from a year ago, which was the last time I saw her."

"Okay. If you say so."

His brow wrinkled in consternation. "Don't do that. Don't mock me."

"I'm not mocking you. I'm accepting what you say, like I did in the past. Of course that video is old. You also never knew where the numbers came from that showed up in your pockets. Brenda was a stalker and you'd never met her before. Oh and sure, all those suggestive photos posted on Gossip Bomb over the years are not you—they're of a guy who looks like you. Right?"

He looked ill, but she didn't care how pitiful he came across. She'd seen that expression before—contrition and a little bit of fear. Yet she couldn't muster a smidge of sympathy, because it was her heart that was breaking. Not his.

Terrence clasped his hands together. "I admit, I lied to you in the past. A lot. But this time—"

"This time, you're not lying."

"You don't believe me."

"I didn't come here to talk about her."

He frowned. "Then why did you come? You're obviously upset."

"Yes, I'm upset, but I'm not going to waste any more energy on you and your women."

"She's not my woman! *You* are the only woman I've touched or seen since April. Period. No one else. You have to believe me. You really think I would invite you to New Orleans while I was laid up with another woman? While we been working on possibly getting back together?"

She shook her head at him in disgust, refusing to allow the sadness that filled her heart to swallow her whole. "I realized something about myself when I saw that video of you and her walking into the hotel together. I realized that for years I wanted to believe you, but you keep showing me you're not worthy of trust. At some point, I have to get it through my thick skull that you're no good for me."

Terrence closed his eyes. "Don't do this."

"I didn't do this, you did."

He opened his eyes. "She's just out to get me."

"It's always the women's fault, right? You're so innocent."

"No, I'm not innocent, but I'm telling the truth this time."

"Of course you are." She gave him a fake smile. "I came to give you some news, and I need you to be quiet so that I can say what I need to say and leave."

He fell silent.

Charisse licked her lips nervously. "I'm pregnant."

His eyes widened. "You are?" As expected, elation took over his face, and he appeared ready to burst with joy.

She nodded.

"How far along are you?"

"A couple of months." Based on the timeline, she got pregnant in Macon.

"I know what you're thinking, that this baby is a mistake, but it's not. We used to say we wanted four, remember?" he said.

They'd lost their first child—the child she supposedly used to trap him—to a miscarriage. She suddenly wanted to cry and pressed her lips together, focused on a point beyond his shoulder because she couldn't look at him. "We used to say we wanted a lot of things."

Terrence took a step closer. "We can still have that. All of it. Everything we said we wanted," he said urgently.

She dared to look at him and saw the earnest plea in his eyes.

"This baby is a sign," he said. "A sign that we should be together and stop sneaking around like we're doing something wrong. A sign that we can make our relationship work again, no matter what obstacles come our way."

"A sign?" Charisse scoffed. "Yes, it's a sign. A sign that we were careless. We're not kids. We're adults and should have known better."

"I don't regret it. If that's what you want, then you can forget it."

She glared at him. "Does anything get to you at all? Do you care about anybody else but Terrence Burrell?"

He reared back like she'd struck him. "That's unfair."

"No it's not."

"Yes, it is!" he snarled. "You think nothing gets to me? *You* get to me. When I can't see you, when I can't hear your voice..." He shook his head. "You're my world, but you don't believe me. We're happy. Don't let this woman split us apart."

"Do you really think my anger is about Brenda or JoJo or any of your side chicks? It's about you, Terrence. You can't keep your penis in your pants."

"I've been faithful to you!"

"For two months!" she screamed. "You can always hang in there for a while, and then you go right back to doing the same bullshit. Four months from now or six months from now or a year from now, there'll be another stripper or model or groupie that I have to contend with. That's our history, and now you expect me to simply accept what you're saying is the truth? That this time is different?"

"This time *is* different, but you don't want to believe me. You don't want to see I've changed. I tell you I love you all the time, and you don't say a word. You don't react, you don't say shit."

"Oh, does that hurt your feelings? You tell me you love me, like you always did, and I'm supposed to fall at your feet and thank my lucky stars that *you love me.*" She shook her head. "You lied to me, you cheated on me, you made a fool out of me.

"What do you know about love? You don't love me. You never loved me. *I loved you*. With everything inside me." Her voice cracked. "I loved you so much, I put up with your bullshit for years while you ran around on me. I loved you so much I didn't care that people said I became pregnant to trap you after you got your record deal. I didn't care because I loved you, and I believed you loved me, too. I used to think your jealousy meant you loved me, but it doesn't. You want to own my body. You see me as a possession, and that's not love. You want to keep me away from Austin and other men and to be the only one to screw me—because that's all you're capable of feeling. Lust. That's it. All you care about is my body, and when that goes you won't want me. You'll be like any other man and trade me in for a newer model."

She wiped the tears from her cheeks, unable to stop saying all the words she'd wanted to say in the past. She'd yelled at him before, but she'd never said these words. "You want to know how I know? You told me in those pathetic songs you wrote for me." She laughed-cried for a minute and then sniffed. "One of your greatest hits was supposed to be a song about me, and I hated it so much.

"You hold the key to my heart

Those other girls don't mean a thing

You hold the key to my heart, sweetheart

You the one wearing my ring."

Before he told her he'd written the song for her, the ad-libbed *sweetheart* at the end of several lines signaled the song was about her. In all the years they'd been together, she'd never heard him call another soul sweetheart. That endearment was uniquely assigned to her.

"And then my other favorite, 'Bomb Pussy.' Oh god. When you wrote that I thought it was sexy and funny. We were still in the honeymoon stage, but later, I hoped that no one knew it was about me, but of course everyone knew."

She picked up her purse. "I'm not saying you're incapable of love. I know you loved Grandma Esther. I know you love our children. But you never loved me, Terrence. Maybe someday you'll learn to love someone the way I did you. Our relationship was good for those first couple of years. Maybe you'll experience that again one day, and the person you love will love you back and treat you the way you deserve. But it won't be me. I did love you, more than anything and anyone, but I can't go down that road with you. I gave you *all* of me, and I can't risk doing that again."

She placed a hand over her belly. "I want this baby, and one day we can talk about it. One day when we're not so emotional—when *I'm* not so emotional." She gave a little laugh.

His face remained solemn and his eyes bleak. Not once did he open his mouth to interrupt while she spoke.

"I'm sorry, Terrence. Take the kids wherever you want, but I can't do any more summer trips with you. I can't sleep with you anymore, and I don't want to look at you or hear your voice for a while. I allowed you to treat me that way, but I won't again. We're done."

She walked out without a backward glance.

## 16

Terrence sat with his feet propped on the coffee table and a beer growing warm in the hand resting on the sofa beside him. In less than six months he went from the high of the Grammys to the depths of hell.

His grandmother passed away and reconnecting with his ex-wife turned out to be the worst decision he had ever made. He would have been better off not making love to her again. Not enjoying her scent. Not touching her, not whispering words of love and dealing with the crushing disappointment when she didn't whisper them back.

Over the past couple of weeks, he'd thrown himself into work at the studio, his escape. He spent long days and nights writing and recording, which kept his mind off his self-inflicted misery. Yet the *Annihilation* album was nowhere close to being finished. The songs were subpar and the lyrics rudimentary at best.

The kids spent time with him only once during the two-week period, when he took them to a movie premiere. He recorded a couple of songs on the soundtrack and played a small role in the film. It was the first time his children walked the red carpet with him, and the pictures from that night—him standing with his two youngest in front and his oldest beside him, still made him smile.

Only one reporter threw out a question about Charisse, which he ignored. Otherwise, the curiosity surrounding their lives fizzled into oblivion, replaced by the next hot topic du jour.

He missed Charisse, but he stayed away, at least for now. He had questions about her health and the baby, but she'd made it clear she didn't want to see or hear from him.

He thought back to that Sunday—the teary eyes, the pain in her voice. Yes, he was jealous and possessive. He did want to keep her body for himself, but that was not all. He wanted her smile and laughter for himself. Her kindness and her big heart and her lasagna for himself. But she wouldn't believe that because his past actions spoke way louder than words.

Hearing her talk about her feelings in the past tense was soul crushing. She said she *did* love him. She had *loved* him. But he killed her love after years of abusing her trust and mistreating her, instead of cherishing her like the jewel he knew her to be. Now the years stretched out before him like a bottomless pit with no end in sight.

Sipping the tepid beer, he watched a mother sob into a microphone on the late-night news. Her tear-filled eyes faced the camera as she begged for her runaway child to come home. "Please come home. Please. I don't know what I'm going to do without you."

He sympathized with the woman. Her words resonated with him.

Without you.

He had everything money could buy—clothes, cars, a SMART condo with every technological advance imaginable. But he didn't have his family. He didn't have Charisse, the love of his life. Without her, his life was nothing.

*Without you.*

He frowned. A beat started in his head and words drifted across his mind's eye.

"There is no me without you," he said to the empty room.

He set the beer on the floor and jumped up from the sofa. He pulled open the drawer of one of the side tables and removed a notepad and pen. He kept them stashed all over the condo for moments like this, when inspiration hit him.

He sat back down and started writing. The words flowed out of him. This was the love song he should've written to her years ago, instead of that other mess he released. He cringed when he thought about the lyrics of "Wearing My Ring." To think that had been his idea of a love song to his wife. To think it became one of his biggest hits. He couldn't count the number of articles that said it showed his softer side. What a joke.

Terrence wrote and wrote. He scratched out a line here, changed a word there, and continued writing.

An hour later, he stopped. He had poured his heart into the song, and it said everything he hadn't been able to say to Charisse. She'd never hear it though. This one he'd keep to himself. But he needed to record it, even if the song never saw the light of day.

Terrence picked up the beer bottle from the floor and dialed Bo's number as he walked to the kitchen.

"Hello?" His friend's groggy voice came over the line.

"What are you doing?"

"Sleep, man. What do you think? I'm in London, remember?" He flew there for the tail end of a hip-hop festival, which meant it was a little after five in the morning.

"I'm sorry, man. I want to get into the studio, and I need you to set it up for me."

"Now?"

"Yes, now."

"What about Kamisha?"

"She's not used to working with the studio people. It'll take her two hours to do what will probably take you fifteen minutes." Terrence emptied the warm beer down the drain and placed the bottle in the recycling bin.

Bo sighed heavily.

"Spare me the attitude. You got this, right?" Terrence asked.

"Yeah, I got this."

"Good. Set it up for me within an hour."

He hung up without waiting for a response. He went into the bedroom and changed into comfortable clothes and a pair of Nikes. Then he exited with the folded pieces of paper tucked into his back pocket.

Within forty-five minutes he entered the studio at the other end of town. Bob, the engineer, was already there and waiting for him.

"This must be pretty important for you to want to meet on such short notice in the middle of the night," Bob said when he came in. He wore a plaid shirt and his hat turned backwards. "I did the usual set up for you."

Terrence sat beside him. "This is gonna be a little different."

"You don't want the Boomer joint?" Bob asked, referring to the track Terrence listened to during the last studio session.

"Nah, I want the other one."

Bob frowned. "Wait... You mean the slow one?"

"Yeah, that one."

Bob shook his head. "A'ight."

He ran the track and Terrence closed his eyes and absorbed the beat. This would definitely do.

Minutes later he was inside the booth, hand on the mic, recording what he considered to be one of his best songs. Title: Without You.

When he exited the booth, he listened to the replay with Bob. At the end of the song, the engineer nodded appreciatively. "That's hot. And you nailed it on the first take. Maybe we should send this one to the record company, give them an early taste of what's to come."

Terrence stood. "I'm not sure I'll put this on the album."

"What? That shit is fire. The ladies are gonna love it. It could be even hotter than 'Wearing My Ring.'"

"We'll see." No point in explaining that it was personal and not for public consumption. He didn't know why, but he'd felt compelled to record the song anyway. "Send that to me after you clean it up."

"Okay."

"Tonight."

"I got you."

"Thanks, man." He tapped Bob on the shoulder and left the building.

Not happier, but satisfied.

## 17

Who could be calling at this hour?

Charisse didn't know the exact time, but she knew it was late because she went to bed at ten o'clock after talking to her mother for an hour. She must've been asleep for at least a couple of hours because her body carried the ache of being disrupted from deep sleep.

She squinted into the darkness and reached for the phone beside the bed. It stopped ringing.

She flopped onto her back and groaned. Whoever had called, they could leave a voicemail and she'd check it in the morning.

Except, the phone started ringing again. Annoyed, she slammed her hand on the offending electronic device and stared at the screen.

Bo?

She answered. "Hello?"

"Oh, thank goodness!"

"What's going on?"

"I hate to ask you for this favor, but I tried to reach Kamisha and she's not answering her phone. I don't know who else to call. It's about T."

Wide awake now, Charisse sat up and gripped the phone as she waited for him to continue.

"A cop picked him up outside the gate at Waterfall Estates. He left his car on the side of the road and tried to enter on foot when the security guard called the police."

"What was he doing there?" Waterfall Estates was the gated community where they'd lived before the divorce.

"I don't know. The guard didn't recognize him, thought he was some random drunk dude trying to force his way onto the property. T has a little bit of cash on him, but no wallet or I.D. They could have arrested him for public drunkenness, but the cop recognized him, took him down to the station, and gave him the chance to make a phone call."

She pressed a hand to her forehead. "Why did you call me?"

"Because I'm in Europe, and if I call anybody else, we risk the incident leaking to the press. Aside from the fact that he don't need any more negative press, he don't need to be seen as getting preferential treatment."

"Even though that's exactly what happened?"

"Yes." Bo sounded defeated, as if he fully expected her to say no.

Charisse sighed. "Which station is he at?"

He told her and gave her the name of the sergeant, adding, "Thanks a lot, Charisse. I know he's not your responsibility, but I really appreciate you doing this. And I know Terrence will, too."

She climbed out of bed. She needed to tell Ennis that she would be leaving him in charge when she left. "Are you sure about that?"

"I'm one hundred percent sure. I don't know how he'll react when he sees you, but trust me, it's better that you go than anyone else. He knows that, too."

She stopped outside her son's door. "Okay, Bo. I'm on my way."

They both hung up.

Why was she going? Because despite what happened between

them, she didn't want him to "give them reporters nothing to write about."

She knocked lightly on the door and walked in to talk to her son.

☙❧

CHARISSE HATED POLICE STATIONS. EVEN WHEN THE OFFICERS WERE friendly, they intimidated her because of the amount of power they wielded. She approached the officer stapling papers at the front desk, a tall white male with bushy brows.

"Can I help you?" he asked without looking at her.

Charisse cleared her throat and clutched the strap of the purse over her shoulder. "Yes, I'm here to see Terrence Burrell. I was told to ask for Sgt. Desmond."

He looked up at her and frowned slightly, as if he wanted to say something. "Down the hall, take a right, last office on the right."

"Thank you."

She followed the instructions and ended up in front of an open office filled with cubicles. A black woman sat at the front of the room at a large desk. Terrence sat in a chair against the wall to the right of the desk, facing Charisse. His head rested against the wall and his eyes were closed. He wore jeans, tennis shoes, and a white tee. She doubted he was asleep, but he remained as still as someone who was. He looked tired and worn, and her heart ached.

"May I help you?" The black officer looked directly at Charisse.

"Are you Sgt. Desmond?"

Terrence's eyes flew open and he sat up straight.

"Yes."

"I'm here for Terrence Burrell."

The sergeant stood with a pen in one hand and rested the other hand on her hip. "Next time a few autographs won't keep him out of jail," she said, arching an eyebrow.

"Yes, ma'am. I understand," Charisse replied, as if she were somehow responsible for the position Terrence found himself in.

"You're free to go," she said to Terrence.

"Thank you." He stood slowly, carefully. As he approached, Charisse noted his red eyes. He looked like he hadn't slept in days.

She followed him out the door. He walked slowly and appeared a bit unsteady on his feet.

"I guess Bo called you?" he said when they were outside the precinct.

"Yes."

"Thanks for coming, but he shouldn't have done that."

"He did what he always does. He had your back."

In the car, Terrence closed his eyes and turned his head away from her toward the window. They didn't speak the entire time they rode to his condo. She pulled into the underground parking garage and into his space.

"Where are the kids?" he asked.

"At home with Ennis. Where's your car?"

"Towed. I'll pick it up tomorrow."

"Do you need anything?"

"No. Thanks for the lift." He opened the door and stumbled out.

Charisse hopped out of the car and stood uncertainly for a bit, not sure whether to go or make sure he actually made his way up to his condo and into bed. She chose the latter. A few more minutes wouldn't hurt. She followed him to the elevator.

Terrence pushed the button and didn't look at her as she came up beside him. "I'll be fine, Charisse."

"I'm sure you will be, but I'm coming up anyway."

They remained silent in the cabin, and when Terrence fumbled with the keycards at the door, she took them from him, found the correct one, and let them in.

"You can go now. I'll be fine."

He tripped over his own feet and she rushed to him. She

caught his arm and supported him before he fell. "You're not fine," she said.

He glanced at her and a pained expression came over his face before he looked away again.

She put his arm around her neck and walked with him down the hall, supporting his big body as best she could, which wasn't easy.

In the bedroom, he flopped onto the mattress, fully clothed, shoes and all.

He heaved a heavy sigh and closed his eyes.

"Are you sure you don't need anything?" Charisse asked. She was worried about him. What if he threw up and drowned in his own vomit or something? She would never forgive herself.

Terrence mumbled something unintelligible into the pillow.

"What did you say?" Charisse leaned over the bed and angled her ear to his mouth.

He grasped her wrist and she gasped at the sudden movement.

They were eye to eye, faces only inches apart.

"Don't go."

She turned her fingers into a fist, ready to jerk away. "I can't stay. I have to go back and see about the kids."

"They'll be fine. Ennis will make sure they're okay. He's old enough to watch out for his brother and sister. The house won't burn down. Call and let him know where you are. Keep your phone on, and lay down with me. I promise I won't try anything. I feel like shit right now, and I..." He swallowed. "You can leave when I fall asleep. I just want to hold you for a little bit."

He released her, giving her the option to go or stay.

Charisse called herself every kind of fool, but she chose to stay.

She removed her shoes and sat on the edge of the bed. She called her son and told him where she was and that she'd see them in the morning. Then she and Terrence slid under the covers. He pulled her close, holding her tight from behind. He threw a leg over both of hers. He said she could leave when he fell asleep, but he was sure making it hard.

He pressed his nose to the back of her neck and breathed deeply, as if saving and filing away her scent for a later date.

"I have something to tell you," he said softly.

"Okay," she replied warily, tension entering her body.

"I don't want you to interrupt or say anything, even after I finish. Just listen. I need to say this for me. Okay?"

Tears filled her eyes, and she blinked them away rapidly. Whatever he was about to say would change their relationship forever. "Okay."

Terrence took a deep breath and let it out through his mouth, and warm air brushed the back of her neck.

"I understand why you didn't believe that I loved you, but in all these years, I thought you knew that I did. If there was one thing that was true during our marriage, it's that I loved you—even though my actions didn't reflect it. I still love you, and I miss you. I miss you more than you know. And I'm sorry for all the shit I've done over the years. For tonight, too. You shouldn't have to come pick me up at the police station.

"I'm sorry for the way I treated you and disrespected you. I'm sorry for destroying what we had as a couple. Sorry for destroying our family and for hurting you and embarrassing you. I'm sorry for everything. Your mother told me you were too good for me, and she was right.

"I want you back, but the truth is, you were right to turn me down. You're a good woman, Charisse, and you put up with a whole lot of my bad behavior. I was listening to something—a song tonight, and it hit me hard. That's what drove me to drink. I realized that I don't deserve you. I want you to know that I get it, sweetheart. I understand why you said no—why you couldn't try again. But you'll always have my heart. Always, whether you want it or not."

He kissed the back of her neck and spread his fingers over her belly. Within minutes, he was snoring, but she couldn't sleep.

She stayed awake for hours, thinking about what he said.

## ❧ 18 ❦

Charisse finished splashing water on her face and walked out of the bathroom. She'd stayed with Terrence until morning broke and left him sleeping in the bed a few minutes ago. She finger-combed her hair, which didn't look too bad considering how she slept last night.

She walked into the kitchen and opened the refrigerator. The shelves were stocked with a variety of food and drinks, including a couple of covered dishes that looked like leftovers from chef-prepared meals.

She could cook a quick breakfast for them, but she needed tomato juice and hot sauce for her hangover drink. She took Terrence's keycards off the side table where she tossed them last night and exited the condo. The market in the building was already open, and she purchased the ingredients she needed.

When she returned upstairs, she checked in on Terrence, who remained sprawled on his stomach in the bed. She watched him for a moment. After what he said last night, maybe they could go back to the friendship they shared before everything fell apart. How the new baby would influence their relationship going forward, she wasn't sure. She was sure, however, that she missed him.

She set up the ingredients on the counter in the kitchen and took the blender from the cabinet. She chopped celery and dropped the pieces into the jar. She poured in tomato juice, hot sauce, and added the other ingredients. Terrence always complained about her hangover recipe, but back in the day when they partied together, the drink always made them feel better the morning after.

She blended the ingredients, did a quick taste test, and satisfied, set the blender aside. Time for breakfast. She was in the mood for an omelette, and Terrence had a couple of mangoes she could slice and add to the side. Before she started, she wanted to play some music. She went over to the sofa and picked up the remote, which looked like a giant keyboard that could be used to control a space ship.

Terrence and his gadgets. This thing was so complicated. Which one controlled the music again?

She walked back to the kitchen, pressing buttons as she went. The TV came on and off. Then the blinds opened and closed.

"Maybe you won't hear any music today," she murmured to herself.

She stood next to one of the bar stools and pushed another button. A song came on with a slow, easy beat. Then Terrence's voice rapped over the beat. She'd never heard this song before. It must be something new he was working on. He sometimes asked the engineer to send him the music to listen to when he was working on an album. *Was the whole album on here?* she wondered.

She walked around the counter and went back to chopping onions when one line in the song stopped her cold.

What's my life without you, sweetheart?

Sweetheart? That was Terrence's word for her. She stared at the controller, as if to make it answer for the music coming through the speakers. She dropped the knife to the cutting board and listened to his deep voice make love to the track with his words.

I ain't got nothing without you

Enough ain't enough without you

There is no me without you
My arms are so empty without you
The sun don't shine without you
It's always night without you
My heart don't beat without you
Just can't breathe without you

By the time the song ended, her cheeks were wet and she sat on one of the barstools because she couldn't stand anymore.

This song…what did it mean? Terrence wrote this song for her. Right? Was this the song he was listening to last night? The one that made him finally accept they would never be a couple again?

Charisse dried her cheeks with a paper towel and then figured out how to turn off the system. She went back to cooking breakfast, mind racing, wondering if there was a chance for them after all.

TERRENCE WALKED BAREFOOT INTO THE WIDE OPEN SPACE OF THE living room. He squinted against the sun and the way it exacerbated his headache. Was the sun always this bright in the morning?

"Good morning. How do you feel?" Charisse asked. She looked bright-eyed and had probably been awake for hours.

"Like crap. How'd you sleep?"

"Good." She held out a glass of brown-looking liquid and he groaned.

"You know I hate this." He took the drink anyway.

"It's good for you, and it works." She handed him two aspirin. "I made breakfast."

"You didn't have to do that."

They were having a very civil conversation, which he appreciated. If for no other reason, they needed to get along for the sake of their kids.

"Sorry about last night." He dry-swallowed the aspirin and sniffed the hangover drink. It smelled like a spicy vegetable smoothie, and he wanted none of it, but she was right, it worked. Holding his breath, he swallowed a large amount of the thick beverage.

He set the half full glass on the counter. Charisse was staring at him.

"What?" he asked.

"Why were you at Waterfall Estates last night?"

"I don't know. Drunk and living in the past. I'm sorry you had to pick me up."

In the light of morning, he was more than embarrassed by his actions. He'd been reckless and could have hurt himself or someone else. But listening to "Without You" in a constant loop destroyed him. Broke him down into an empty vessel. His own words drove home the hopelessness of his situation, and so he'd felt compelled to go there, back to the house where they had lived together as a family under one roof.

Charisse's lower lip trembled, and he clenched his fists, wanting to grab and hold her, but knowing he didn't have the right. "I'm sorry. I know I messed up again, sweetheart—"

She covered her face and sobbed louder now.

Dammit. He'd really screwed up now.

"I'm sorry. I'm sorry." He wrapped her in his arms. He rubbed her back and whispered in her ear, "It's okay."

He closed his eyes and took a moment to appreciate her soft, feminine form and the sweetness of her scent. If he could keep her here forever, he would.

Charisse eased back and he released her. She wiped away the tears.

"You called me sweetheart," she said. More tears spilled from her eyes, and she wiped them away with the back of her hand.

"Yeah...?" He didn't understand what she was getting at.

"I'm the only one you call sweetheart...right?"

He'd never really thought about it before, but that was true. Chelsea was his princess, and other women he called babe or baby, assuming he used an affectionate name for them at all.

"Yeah. Because you're the only one. You're my sweetheart." He brushed a thumb across her cheek and wiped away a fat tear that fell.

"I'm not upset. I... I heard the new song for the album. It's about me, isn't it?" Her tear-filled eyes searched his. She asked the question, but she feared the answer.

"Yes, but it's not for the album. I'm not going to release it."

"I want you to release it. It's beautiful."

He studied her for a moment and then took both of her hands in his. "Did you really listen to the words? I meant everything I said. I'm nothing without you. Nothing."

She gave him a watery smile. "About what you said last night, before you fell asleep..."

Terrence shook his head. "We don't have to talk about that. I needed to say those things to you for me. I needed you to know, that's all."

"Well, I have something to say to you, too."

He braced for the words about to come out of her mouth.

"You're right, you don't deserve me. You were awful to me."

He didn't react.

"But I want to be with you. I turned over everything you said in my head and considered all we'd been through. Losing our first child. Our marriage. Your career successes. Everything. And then this song... I... I believe you. Maybe I'm crazy, and I hope this isn't a mistake, but I want to try again."

Terrence couldn't breathe. He wanted to be happy but worried she was giving him another chance for the wrong reason. "If you're doing this because you feel sorry for me, don't."

"I didn't say that because I feel sorry for you. I said it because... When things are good between us, they're really, really good, and you make me happier than anyone else. You take good care of me, and you're an excellent father. I want to be with you, and I want to be with you because I love you. You have my heart, too, Terrence. You didn't take good care of it before, but I believe you will now, and I'm willing to take a chance on us."

"And you forgive me?" he asked thickly, voice shaking.

"Yes, I forgive you."

The words were barely out of her mouth before he flung his arms around her and lifted her from the floor in a tight bear hug. She laughed, cupping the back of his head with both hands and wrapping her legs around his waist. She dropped soft little kisses to his nose and cheeks.

Terrence looked deeply into her eyes. "You won't regret it. I promise. I love you so much. Thank you, thank you for giving me another chance. I won't screw it up this time, I promise. I'll be the best husband you could ever have. I'm going to love you so much and so hard. I'll show you every day. You gon' be sick of my ass."

"I can't wait," Charisse whispered.

"Yeah, baby!" he bellowed, tossing his head back.

She laughed, her grin broad and bright. That was the same look she wore on their wedding day—as if she'd snagged the biggest prize. But he was the one who'd snagged a prize.

"You're stuck with me now," he said against her lips.

Then he kissed her. Hard.

# EPILOGUE

Terrence sat on the side of the pool writing in his notebook. Sunglasses shielded his eyes as the Hawaiian sun doused his family playing in the pool. Almost a year had passed since he and Charisse reconciled, and the ensuing months exceeded his expectations.

They got married in the gazebo on the newly landscaped grounds of the house, in a small private ceremony that included only close family and friends. Martha attended with her new beau but remained skeptical about them remarrying. Terrence was still working on convincing her that he was worthy of her daughter, but he was up to the challenge.

When the officiant said, "You may kiss the bride," he wrapped one arm around Charisse's neck and kissed her, and kissed her, and kissed her until Bo yelled, "Let her breathe, T. Damn!"

They never issued a formal announcement to the public. Charisse simply started showing up to events with him, and when the press took note of the rings on their fingers, they figured it out.

The stories about their reunion were overwhelmingly positive, and some of the social media comments were interesting and funny.

*Why you put him through all that? You know he loved you, girl.*

*Beautiful family #goals*

*What a beautiful sight. #blacklove*

Of course, not everyone thought their reunion was a good idea.

*I give it six months and he'll be cheating on her again.*

*Some women never learn. LMAO*

*So dumb. He hasn't changed. Guess she gonna learn the hard way. SMDH.*

Sales of *Annihilation* surpassed his previous works. The first release, "Without You," was a huge hit and set the tone for what critics called a more mature album. Terrence won Album of the Year at the Grammys, and this time Charisse was right there, blowing him kisses and beaming proudly from the audience.

In a couple of weeks, he started rehearsals for the next tour. Fans snatched up tickets fast since they knew this was the last one before retirement. Ennis had decided to take a gap year before he started at Morehouse and planned to travel around the world with him while he toured.

Another big change in the past year was the birth of their daughter, who currently slept under the watchful gaze of the nanny. No one was more enamored with her than her big sister, Chelsea, who made plans to teach her everything she knew about being a princess.

"Come on in the water, baby. Are you going to stay out there writing all day?" Charisse pouted but resumed playing volleyball with their kids. She wore an aqua blue one piece that looked amazing against her skin, which had darkened to a toastier brown after days in the Hawaiian sun.

"One minute." Terrence wrote a few more lines, noting his thoughts before they were gone. He could perfect the words later, but these verses were a start. He may never share them, but it felt good to write about the joy he felt every day ever since he reunited with his family.

He set aside the notebook and removed his sunglasses. Then he took a running leap toward the pool. "Incoming!" he yelled, and executed a perfect cannonball into the water, eliciting screams and shouts from everyone else.

He waded over to Charisse. "I'm on Mommy's side."

"No fair," Chelsea said. "You'll beat us."

"There are three of you and two of us. Bring it." Out the corner of his mouth, he whispered, "We're kicking their asses."

His wife giggled and shook her head.

*His wife.* Charisse was his wife again.

Her laughter, genuine happiness, and beauty blew him away. Every day he marveled at being given a second chance. Being given the opportunity to make her happy, to wake up next to this amazing woman. Older and wiser, he would never squander his chance again. He was too damn appreciative he actually received one.

He looped an arm around her neck and kissed her cheek. She beamed up at him with water droplets on her smooth skin. He kissed her soft lips, which were his to kiss whenever he wanted, as long as they both shall live. Charisse moaned, teasing him with a little bit of tongue.

*Bump.*

The beach ball bounced against the side of Terrence's head. He tore his mouth away from Charisse and glared across the pool at his three laughing children. The boys gave Chelsea a high five.

"Great shot," Junior said.

"That was you, princess?" Terrence said in his best wounded voice.

"That's what you get," Chelsea replied. "You kiss Mommy all the time. This is volleyball time, not kissing time."

"Oh, it's like that? Okay, get ready, cause it's on."

He picked up the ball and launched it across the water with a powerful serve. With lots of laughter and splashing around, an energetic game of water volleyball commenced.

And there was nowhere else Terrence Burrell would rather be.

# JOHNSON FAMILY SERIES

For more Black romance, check out the Johnson Family series—about a billionaire beer and restaurant dynasty based in Seattle. Meet Ivy, Cyrus, Trenton, Gavin, and Xavier in Unforgettable, Perfect, Just Friends, The Rules, and Good Behavior.

# ALSO BY DELANEY DIAMOND

**Quicksand**

- A Powerful Attraction
- Without You

**Royal Brides**

- Princess of Zamibia

**Brooks Family series**

- Passion Rekindled
- Do Over
- Wild Thoughts

**Love Unexpected series**

- The Blind Date
- The Wrong Man
- An Unexpected Attraction
- The Right Time
- One of the Guys
- That Time in Venice

**Johnson Family series**

- Unforgettable
- Perfect
- Just Friends
- The Rules
- Good Behavior

**Latin Men series**

- The Arrangement
- Fight for Love
- Private Acts
- The Ultimate Merger
- Second Chances
- More Than a Mistress
- Undeniable
- Hot Latin Men: Vol. I (print anthology)
- Hot Latin Men: Vol. II (print anthology)

**Hawthorne Family series**

- The Temptation of a Good Man
- A Hard Man to Love
- Here Comes Trouble
- For Better or Worse
- Hawthorne Family Series: Vol. I (print anthology)
- Hawthorne Family Series: Vol. II (print anthology)

**Bailar series** (sweet/clean romance)

- Worth Waiting For

**Stand Alones**

- A Passionate Love
- Still in Love
- Subordinate Position
- Heartbreak in Rio

**Other**

- Audiobooks

- Free Stories

# ABOUT THE AUTHOR

Delaney Diamond is the USA Today Bestselling Author of sweet, sensual, passionate romance novels. Originally from the U.S. Virgin Islands, she now lives in Atlanta, Georgia. She reads romance novels, mysteries, thrillers, and a fair amount of nonfiction. When she's not busy reading or writing, she's in the kitchen trying out new recipes, dining at one of her favorite restaurants, or traveling to an interesting locale.

Enjoy free reads and the first chapter of all her novels on her website. Join her mailing list to get sneak peeks, notices of sale prices, and find out about new releases.

Join her mailing list
www.delaneydiamond.com

f facebook.com/DelaneyDiamond

🐦 twitter.com/DelaneyDiamond

📌 pinterest.com/DelaneyDiamond

Made in the USA
Middletown, DE
23 August 2019